MW00478518

A Notion to Murder

A Southern Quilting Mystery, Volume 16

Elizabeth Craig

Published by Elizabeth Craig, 2022.

A NOTION TO MURDER

First edition. April 19, 2022.

Written by Elizabeth Craig.

Chapter One

B eatrice gratefully took a sip of her coffee. She was at June Bug's bakery and it was quite early in the morning. Sometimes Beatrice was an early riser and sometimes she slept a good deal longer than she intended to. But today she was sitting with her friend, Posy, at the bakery before Posy had to open her quilt shop, The Patchwork Cottage, for the morning. The sun was coming up and the clouds looked like cotton candy in the sunrise over the mountains.

Posy also seemed a little sleepy, despite the fact the early hour was part of her regular routine. She gave Beatrice a smile. "Maybe a little sugar will help wake us up."

Beatrice quirked an eyebrow. "Should we doctor our coffees? Mine already has a generous amount of sugar in it."

"No, I mean we should get doughnuts. Maybe the powdered sugar ones." Posy's eyes lit up at the thought.

Beatrice had the feeling that would definitely wake her up. However, when she was on sugar highs, she found herself crashing later on, often at inopportune times. "Maybe we should go with just a *little* sugar. Like a muffin."

Posy looked over at the display counter, her blue eyes wide. "The blueberry ones looked amazing, didn't they? Blueberries were practically popping out of them. And they had some sort of sugary topping on them." Posy was clearly completely focused on the thought of sugar.

Rowesa, who was June Bug's worker, grinned at them. "It's a sugary cinnamon crumb topping." Rowesa's daughter and June Bug's niece had become fast friends and so had Rowesa and June Bug. Since they were both solo caregivers, they helped each other out by watching the kids.

The delicious description of the blueberry muffins convinced Beatrice and Posy that they both wanted one. Or one to start out with. They looked to Beatrice like the kind of muffins that might quickly multiply on her plate as she went back for seconds or thirds.

"Where is June Bug this morning?" Beatrice asked Rowena casually as she rang them up.

"Oh, she's making a birthday cake delivery."

Beatrice said, "I didn't realize June Bug was still making deliveries. I'd think folks would just come in to pick up their order."

Rowena nodded. "Usually, that's the way it goes. But she still delivers the bigger cakes—wedding cakes, for sure. And this particular cake had enough layers that the family asked if she could deliver it. I totally get it—I've transported cakes before and they slid all over my car and ruined them. But June Bug has her method for doing it. She makes sure the cake is secured to the platter with extra buttercream icing. Actually, she uses more than one cake board to make sure it's really stable. Then she puts the box on a yoga mat on the floor of the car."

"A yoga mat," said Beatrice. "I'd have never thought of that."

"Who's having the major birthday?" asked Posy. "It sounds like someone is having a big party."

"It's for Lester Dawson," said Rowena, but she said it more like a question. "I don't think I know him. It was a pretty elaborate cake, though. You know how beautiful June Bug's cakes are. He's turning eighty-five."

"Mercy," said Posy mildly.

Beatrice and Posy settled back at their table as the door opened and another customer came in. Beatrice said, "So Posy, do you have anything fun coming up? I need some ideas. Wyatt and I need to shake things up a little bit. I think we've gotten wedged into our routine. It would be great if he and I could do some short trips or something. Maybe just a couple of days away."

Posy's bright blue eyes widened. "Oh, I forgot to tell you. Cork and I are planning a big anniversary trip. We're going to go to Yellowstone and the Grand Tetons!"

"That sounds wonderful, Posy! I know you and Cork are huge nature lovers. You should really be able to see some great wildlife over there. How much planning is the trip taking?"

Posy said, "Well, we started months ago."

Beatrice opened her eyes wide. "Really? It takes that much planning?"

"Just one part of it does. To get reservations to stay inside the national park you have to make them right when they open them up to the public or they're already gone. So we got our lodging reservations and our plane tickets a long time ago. But now we're making lists of our top places to see and where we should eat and that sort of thing. It looks like such a fun trip. You know how we love sitting out on our deck and watching the birds and the deer in our yard. This will be watching animals on a *big* scale."

Beatrice said wistfully, "Getting away sounds wonderful right now."

"You and Wyatt should do it!" Posy thought for a moment. "Why don't you come with us? We'd have so much fun."

Beatrice chuckled. "We wouldn't dream of interrupting a romantic trip, Posy. It's your anniversary."

"It's not *that* romantic. It's Cork." Posy had a mischievous smile on her face that made Beatrice laugh again. Cork wasn't exactly anyone's idea of a romantic hero with his crusty manner and bald head. But he was kind, and he and Posy always got along marvelously together and had many of the same interests.

"Just the same, I think Wyatt and I will have to dream up our own trip. Maybe we'll make it to Yellowstone one day, but I don't see us making that trip anytime soon. The main problem is that it's so hard to get Wyatt away from Dappled Hills."

Posy nodded in an understanding way. Wyatt was the minister of the Dappled Hills Presbyterian church. There weren't any associate ministers (there had temporarily been one, but he'd moved on to another church in a different town) so Wyatt was kept very busy with their active church. If Wyatt took time off, he called up a substitute minister from a nearby town. It wasn't the perfect solution, at least not to Beatrice. She felt a little selfish, but she'd like to not have to share Wyatt with the congregation *quite* as much as she did.

"Wyatt always does such a wonderful job with the services and all the activities at the church," said Posy. "And the Bible studies and youth group and mission trips."

"I have a feeling there's a *but* coming," said Beatrice dryly.

"It's just that some of us worry a little over him. Are we all burning him out? I do fret over it, Cork can tell you. On top of all the regular, weekly duties, there are those *unexpected* duties, too."

Beatrice nodded. "The weddings."

"And the funerals. Sometimes I think the funerals are more complicated than the weddings."

"You're thinking the church should be looking for another associate minister," said Beatrice.

Posy quickly added, "We all think Wyatt is just perfect! But, well, he's not getting any younger and surely he would like to have more opportunity to just stop and smell the roses once in a while."

Beatrice reached out and gave Posy's hand a quick squeeze. "Right you are, Posy. Thank you. I think that's a subject I should bring up with Wyatt soon."

Posy said, "After all, you want to spend as much fun time with your little grandbaby as you can. You could go to the beach with him—that would be so much fun. Building sandcastles, splashing in the waves. That wouldn't keep Wyatt away from the church for too long and it would be a nice break for you. How is Will doing, by the way? I bet he's growing like a weed."

Beatrice chuckled. "Lucky for you that you're talking with me and not Meadow. Meadow would have a slideshow presentation prepared about our co-grandson. And, yes, he's doing great, thanks. He's doing a little better with his talking now."

Posy's bright blue eyes twinkled. "Adorable. The last time he was in the shop, he was saying 'no' a lot."

"Yes, I think he's mastered that word," said Beatrice dryly. "He's trying really hard to get my name right. My Grandmother Name, I mean."

"Oh, what's your grandma name?" Posy tilted her head to one side. "Somehow I can't quite picture what you might pick out as your name."

Beatrice grinned at her. "I think I might like to hear what you come up with before I share it."

"Okay." Posy peered closely at Beatrice as if the answer might be written somewhere on her face. "Mimi? No, never mind. I can't really picture you as a Mimi. Nana?"

Beatrice shook her head. "Try again."

Posy lit up. "Oh, I know! Grandmama."

"You got it!" said Beatrice, looking a little surprised.

"Well, there are only so many names. Plus, Piper calls you mama, so it was a good guess."

"Very perceptive of you, Posy. Unfortunately, Will hasn't quite figured it out yet. He's been mangling it in the cutest of ways. He wrinkles his little nose and blurts out something really garbled. Maybe 'amma' or 'granna'. It doesn't consistently seem to be one thing."

Posy asked, "Is that happening with Meadow, too?"

Beatrice made a face. "No, and it's maddening. I'm convinced that Meadow has a recording of her saying 'granny' that she plays over and over while Will naps."

Beatrice's cell phone rang and she pulled it quickly from her purse. She frowned. "It's June Bug . . . that's odd."

When Beatrice answered, June Bug started breathlessly apologizing for calling so early.

"No worries at all. I'm actually here with Posy at your shop," said Beatrice.

June Bug, her voice relieved, said, "Oh good. I'm so sorry but . . . could you come pick me up? I'd ask Rowena, but she's watching the shop."

"Of course I can," said Beatrice, fumbling to remove her keys from her purse. "Are you at home?"

"I'm at Lester Dawson's house," said June Bug, sounding very distracted and still rather breathless.

"Oh, right—Rowena said you were making a cake delivery there." Beatrice paused. "Is everything all right?"

June Bug said in a wavering voice, "No. No, it's not. Lester Dawson is dead!"

Chapter Two

It didn't take long for Beatrice to toss her trash away, quickly fill in Posy, and jump into her car. It did take a bit longer on the winding mountain roads to reach the Dawson house. Although perhaps *mansion* or *castle* might be better words for the edifice in front of her. She'd driven past the house before on her way to other places so was generally aware where it was (and her GPS navigated her more exactly.) It was the kind of house you craned your head to catch a glimpse of. You had to peer through a thicket of trees and well-groomed shrubbery to spot anything. Today, however, Beatrice had a front row seat as she pulled up right in front of the house.

She climbed out of the car and stared up at the huge house. It was beautiful in an austere way. But Beatrice didn't find the stone edifice at all homey, especially compared to her small cottage full of comfy, overstuffed sofas and cozy quilts, with soft pillows scattered everywhere.

There were already several emergency vehicles there with lights flashing, although there weren't any sirens. But then, there apparently wasn't an emergency if Lester was dead. The stone mansion loomed above them with turrets and even a couple of grinning gargoyles. Beatrice looked around for June Bug, but didn't immediately see the small woman.

She got out of her car and started cautiously walking over, not wanting to get in the way of the emergency workers. Then she saw Ramsay, the local police chief, turn around and spotted June Bug sitting forlornly on the stone steps in front of him. She was wearing her bakery uniform which was a recent addition to her wardrobe. It was a pink apron with a wooden spoon and "June Bug's Bakery" embroidered on it, over her black top and slacks. Beatrice hadn't quite gotten used to seeing June Bug wearing it yet. She'd always been incredibly professional, no matter if she was cleaning houses or baking, just because of her pure, unequaled efficiency. But her usual outfits had tended to be forest green pants and a white tee shirt.

Ramsay waved her over and Beatrice hurried to join them. Ramsay looked as if he'd gotten ready in a hurry—he'd probably not made it into the small police station yet when the phone call had come in. He was a short man with a receding hairline and kind eyes. He was also a tremendous reader and prolific writer who was looking forward to a well-deserved retirement.

"Glad you could make it," said Ramsay. "June Bug has her car here, of course, but I didn't think she was in fit shape to drive it. I asked her if she could ring a friend."

Beatrice gave June Bug a warm smile. It was always really nice to feel not just useful, but to be thought of as a friend to help in a rough time. "Of course I could come." She paused. "Is it all right for us to go now? Or should we wait?"

Ramsay said, "Maybe you could wait a few minutes? The state police are on their way and they might want a statement."

He gave June Bug a kind look. "Meadow packed me a container of breakfast food and shoved it at me as I was heading out the door. Maybe you'd like one of the country ham biscuits."

June Bug gave him a rather sad smile as if she'd very much like one of Meadow's biscuits . . . under ordinary circumstances. Beatrice thought she looked as if she might appreciate something to settle her stomach, instead.

"Thanks, Ramsay," said Beatrice.

Ramsay walked away to speak with a woman who was wearing all black and looking as though she'd had a shock.

June Bug rallied enough to say, "She's the housekeeper."

"I suppose she's the one who let you in when you came with the cake?"

June Bug nodded, looking at the housekeeper solemnly.

Beatrice guessed that June Bug wouldn't want to talk through what she'd just witnessed for a while so she set about giving an airy narrative about her visit to the bakery, Posy and Cork's upcoming anniversary trip, and anything else that came into her mind. She was glad to see June Bug's color returning as she spoke.

Beatrice was mentally patting herself on the back for her excellent distraction technique when she suddenly noticed a big tear plop on June Bug's round cheek.

"I'm sorry," said Beatrice, wincing. June Bug just looked so sad.

"It was his birthday," said June Bug. "It seems really wrong."

"I know," said Beatrice gently. She sat with June Bug for a few quiet moments before saying, "Had you met Lester . . . before?"

She shook her head sadly. "I'd spoken to the maid on the phone. But Imelda said Lester had picked the cake himself. He never even got to see it."

Beatrice thought it was a little odd that Lester's wife or children didn't order his cake for him. But she supposed it was the best way to ensure you got what you wanted.

June Bug pushed another tear off her cheek and Beatrice dove into her handbag to find her pack of travel tissues, thrusting them at June Bug.

June Bug took them gratefully. After a couple of moments, she said in a trembling voice, "It was awful. Imelda and I didn't know what we were going to see."

"Was Lester in the living room?" Beatrice hesitated. "Or maybe a library? It looks like the kind of house that might have a library." She could imagine a large room full of leather-bound tomes remaining largely unread. Beatrice always thought it was sad when books weren't read and were just used to make a statement. It denied them their intrinsic usefulness.

June Bug considered this. "An office? Study? A room with a desk. A *big* desk."

Beatrice could imagine that, too.

"There were lots of books in there, too," said June Bug in a clear effort to be as accurate as possible.

June Bug was sounding better as she talked, but Beatrice didn't want to make her relive the experience unless she brought it up herself. Which she immediately did.

"Mr. Dawson had been hit on the head," she said solemnly, her round face pale.

Beatrice had originally assumed Lester had suffered some sort of natural death. At the age of eighty-five, it didn't require a stretch of the imagination. She should have been tipped off by the number of policemen who were still arriving at the scene.

"Could it have been an accident?" asked Beatrice slowly. "Maybe he tripped and hit his head on his desk? Or could he have had a heart attack and hit his head as he fell?"

June Bug looked doubtful. "Maybe? But probably not."

That didn't sound good.

June Bug's bug-like eyes opened even wider than usual. "Mellie!" she gasped.

Beatrice looked around in concern. "Is she here?" Mellie was a fellow quilter and Lester's daughter.

June Bug shook her head. "But she's going to be so sad. And it's his *birthday*."

Poor June Bug seemed stuck on this particular angle. She pulled out a fresh tissue as more tears made their way down her round cheeks.

A luxury car pulled up and a bald, mustachioed, taciturn man climbed gravely out of it. Beatrice recognized him as Archibald Dawson, Lester's eldest child. He was very much in-volved in the running of Wyatt's church, having served as an el-der for years. Beatrice didn't know him as well as Wyatt did, but knew he had the reputation of being extremely organized, clever, and the type of elder who got the job done well and in a timely fashion.

Ramsay was still occupied with the housekeeper so Archibald strode over to Beatrice and June Bug, still perched on the front steps.

"Beatrice," said Archibald in his brusque manner. "It's good to see you here. Do you know Wyatt's schedule for the next few days?"

From what she knew of Archibald, she wasn't too startled that he launched immediately into planning the funeral service instead of initiating their conversation with niceties or talking about his deceased father.

Beatrice said, "I only know that Wyatt will certainly move his schedule around to accommodate your father's service. I'm so sorry about this."

Archibald nodded, his shoulders taut with tension. "Thank you. I appreciate that." He gave June Bug a curious look and she gave him a shy, uncertain smile.

Beatrice quickly introduced them, adding, "June Bug was here delivering a birthday cake for your father. Such awful timing."

Beatrice meant that it was awful that Lester's death was apparently on the day of his birth. But Archibald took it to mean that June Bug had bad timing by delivering a cake at a surprisingly tragic time. He looked at the little woman with concern. "It certainly was. Are you all right, then?"

June Bug bobbed her head immediately, looking anxiously down at her hands, never one who liked to be the center of attention.

Archibald looked back over to where Ramsay and the housekeeper were still in conversation. "I suppose Imelda escorted you inside and the two of you made the unfortunate discovery?"

Beatrice noticed he still hadn't referred to his father.

June Bug nodded again. Apparently feeling she needed to further explain she said, "Imelda wanted your dad to approve it."

Archibald pressed his lips together. "I see."

Beatrice said, "Ramsay must have called you right away."

"He did. Ramsay knows that I try to keep tabs on what's going on here at the house. I was planning on heading over here at this time anyway. I like to keep an eye on the grounds and make sure the house is in order."

Beatrice couldn't help but wonder why he thought his father and mother were incapable of doing that. But from what she knew of Archibald's take-charge attitude at the church, she figured that he was just the kind of person who preferred to make sure things met his own standards.

"I don't suppose Ramsay said anything about when the death may have occurred?" This was directed to Beatrice.

Again, no direct mention of his father. Beatrice shook her head. "I'm afraid not."

June Bug shook her head, too.

Archibald leveled his gaze on June Bug again. "So he was still in his bedroom, was he?"

June Bug's eyes grew large and she shook her head again, this time faster. "His office."

"Hmm. So it certainly sounds as though this might have happened last night. My father wasn't much of an early riser. It's not very likely he would have already gotten up this morning and then headed to his office. While I'm here checking in on everything, I often wake him up for the day. Keeping to a routine is important, even for someone his age."

Beatrice was still wanting to hear a bit more about Lester. She said, "It must have been a terrible shock to you. Is there anything Wyatt and I can do to help, aside from helping with the service?"

Archibald seemed to suddenly realize he hadn't been exactly behaving like a grieving son. He said somberly, "Thank you, Beatrice, that's very kind. Nothing immediately comes to mind, but I will certainly contact you if something does." He paused and then said a bit awkwardly, "I suppose I must appear a bit distanced from the whole thing. I'm afraid I'm not much of a sentimental person. I came by it naturally, since neither mother nor father are sentimental. But I did admire my father and will miss him very much. He was a self-made man and there aren't many of those around."

Archibald's lips tightened into a thin line as he looked at something behind Beatrice. She turned to see a woman wandering around the estate.

Beatrice realized she must have a questioning look on her face because Archibald said shortly, "My father's companion." He frowned. "It's a very odd set-up and certainly not one I condoned. Shirley isn't ordinarily at the house. She's usually at her *own* house, which my father paid for. I'd be very interested in knowing what she's doing here."

Beatrice wasn't sure what to say in response to that and was mulling over her options when Archibald said, "Ah. Looks like Ramsay has wrapped up with Imelda. Good to see you Beatrice. And you, too, um . . . " He wasn't quite able to dredge up June Bug's name from his memory, so gave her a bob of his head instead and then strode off to Ramsay.

June Bug looked startled at the coming and going.

"Sort of different here, isn't it?" asked Beatrice mildly.

She was about to urge June Bug to her waiting car when Shirley, Lester's "companion," as Archibald had put it, hurried up to them.

Chapter Three

S hirley, who was 50-ish, was more striking than she was beautiful, with large eyes, big teeth, and asymmetrical features.

"Sorry," she said to Beatrice. "I was going to speak with the police, but they seem tied up right now. Do you know what's going on here?"

Beatrice looked over at Ramsay, thinking that he might rather be the one to tell Shirley about Lester and gauge her response to his death. Ramsay caught her gaze, made what looked like quick excuses to Archibald, and joined them.

"Hi," said Ramsay. "Could you tell me who you are?"

"I'm Shirley Keller. I'm dating Lester, who lives here."

Ramsay blinked a little at her forthrightness. "Dating the married Lester!"

"What he does is his affair," said Shirley with a shrug.

Ramsay wisely decided not to pursue this line of questioning. "Why are you here on the property now?"

Shirley shrugged again. "He didn't show up at my house this morning, as planned."

"What time was he supposed to be there?" asked Ramsay.

"An hour ago. Or even longer, probably."

Ramsay asked, "You didn't try calling him on the phone?"

"He didn't answer. But then, he's eighty-five years old and he sometimes walks away from his phone or doesn't check it. But he is, ordinarily, prompt. So I came by to see what was going on. And I saw all this." Shirley made an expansive motion with her arm to indicate the different emergency vehicles and people milling around. "And now I think you should answer a question for *me*. What's going on here? Where's Lester?"

Ramsay said in a grim voice, "I'm sorry to have to tell you this, but Lester has died."

Shirley didn't seem completely taken aback by this, a fact that Ramsay also noticed and asked her about.

She said, "He was eighty-five years old. Stuff happens when you're in your eighties."

Ramsay shook his head. "Not this time. Lester didn't have a natural death."

Now there was more of a reaction from Shirley.

"Wait. You're saying he was *murdered*?" Her gaze darted around, taking in the police tape for the first time. Then she put her hands up. "Well, I didn't have anything to do with that. Like I said, I came over here a few minutes ago to check on Lester since he didn't show up at my place at our pre-arranged time."

Ramsay said, "Where were you before then?"

"At home, of course! Waiting. I can give you all the boring details. I got up this morning around six, fed the cat, and made myself coffee. Then I caught up with social media on my phone, took a shower, and got ready for the day. After that, I started wondering where Lester was. I hung out for a while at the house, tried calling him, and came over here. End of story."

Shirley folded her arms in front of her and glared at Ramsay.

"Can you tell me what your relationship with Lester was like?" asked Ramsay.

Shirley tilted her head to one side, considering this. "He was actually very kind and thoughtful. That's something I haven't experienced a lot in my life and I really appreciated it. We got along well. He took care of me—he was paying for the house I'm living in." She made a face. "I guess the family probably won't want to keep paying that mortgage." But a cunning gleam came into her eyes and Beatrice wondered if Shirley had a plan to get the money.

"Was it often that Lester didn't make it over to your place when you'd made plans?" asked Ramsay.

"Not at all; that's what I was saying. He was very punctual and felt very strongly about being on time. He was an early riser and so I wondered right away if something was wrong when he didn't make it over."

Beatrice frowned. Archibald had mentioned that his father wasn't fond of a routine and that he often had to wake him up. Did Archibald not know his father as well as he thought?

Ramsay asked slowly, "Were you and Lester very close? There was quite a significant age difference between you. Did you have much in common?"

"We had *plenty* in common. The way we looked at the world was very similar. We're both really driven people who don't have a lot of patience with just sitting around. We make things happen. He cared about me you know."

Ramsay nodded and Shirley apparently wasn't satisfied with this response. "He *did*. He even changed his will to include me in it. He told me so." She gave a devilish smile. "The family won't be happy when they hear that."

"Does Tilda . . . does Lester's wife know about your relationship?"

Shirley said, "Tilda pretty much let Lester do whatever Lester wanted to do. It wasn't as if we were flaunting our affair. We weren't cutting into their family time or Lester's other responsibilities. I think Tilda and Lester lived completely separate lives."

Ramsay jotted down a note in the tiny notebook he was holding. Then he looked at Shirley over his reading glasses. "Since you two were close, do you have any ideas about who might have done this? Did Lester mention anybody who wanted to do him harm? Was he having any trouble with anyone? Had he received any threats?"

"That family should all be suspects," said Shirley flatly.

Ramsay quirked an eyebrow. "I take it you weren't close with the family."

Beatrice hid a smile.

"Not likely." Shirley sniffed. "Anyway, that's the most dysfunctional family you'll see in town. None of them got along with Lester, from what I heard from him. I'm the only one who was really close to him."

Ramsay poised his pencil over the notepad. "Could you elaborate on that? Be specific?"

"Sure. First off, there's Archibald." She peered behind her and saw Archibald staring at her coldly. "I guess he can't hear me, but he knows I'm talking about him, just the same. He likes to think he's the perfect son but Lester knew differently."

"How's that?" Ramsay jotted down Archibald's name.

"Lester was the one who told Archibald's wife that he was cheating on her. Not as perfect as he looks, right? Archibald was furious with Lester over that."

Ramsay said slowly, "What was the reason Lester told her that? Was he trying to break up the two of them?"

Shirley shook her head impatiently. "Why would Lester even care about that? No, what Lester thought was important was the *truth*. He didn't have any patience with secrets."

Beatrice wondered if his liking for exposing secrets had anything to do with Lester's sudden, violent demise.

Ramsay tilted his head to one side, tapping his pencil on the notepad. "What happened when Lester told Archibald's wife about the affair?"

"What do you think happened? She blew up. Now they're separated. It made Archibald livid, according to Lester. Like I said, he likes to act as if he's so perfect. Then Lester showed he wasn't so perfect after all." Shirley smirked.

"Anybody else in the family? You made it sound like a blanket statement indicting all of them." Ramsay quirked his eyebrow again.

"Sure. There's Jack." Shirley paused. "I actually do sort of like Jack. He's younger and fun and isn't like Archibald at all—I don't think he cares about his personal dignity one bit. I feel like he's the kid who was most similar to Lester. He's a straightshooter, too."

"But you think he could possibly be a suspect." It wasn't a question.

Shirley nodded. "Of course. They all could. Just because I like Jack doesn't mean that he didn't have any motive to get rid of his father. Jack is poor as a church mouse and Lester wasn't one for doling out handouts. So there's definitely the money angle there. There was also some kind of secret that Jack had that Lester knew about."

"I thought you were saying that Jack was a straightshooter and wasn't much into secrets."

Shirley frowned at him. "I never said he didn't *have* secrets. I just said he was more like Lester."

"What kind of secret is it?"

Shirley shrugged impatiently. "No idea. Lester kept it to himself, but I think he was using it as leverage to keep Jack in line. Not that Jack always stayed in line. But you'd know that, of course."

Beatrice glanced at Ramsay with interest. Apparently, Jack might be a known entity to the local police department.

"Yes," said Ramsay noncommittally. "Lester had a daughter, too, didn't he?"

Beatrice winced a little. Mellie was a quilter and a friend of hers. She was also a friend of Ramsay's wife, Meadow. Meadow was quite ferocious whenever fellow quilters fell under suspicion.

"Mellie," said Shirley with a nod. "I guess Mellie was probably Lester's favorite. But she and her husband have hit hard times, according to Lester. A little extra money wouldn't hurt, would it? Then there's Tilda." She smirked again.

"Not a huge fan of Tilda's?"

"I just don't know the woman. Our paths really haven't crossed, as you might guess. I'm thinking she might just have been tired of living her life with Lester, though. Wouldn't you think? She probably never dreamed he'd live this long. They've been married for ages."

Ramsay made a few more notes on his notepad.

"Then there's Lester's illegitimate daughter." Shirley gave a sly smile as if realizing she was dropping a bombshell.

Beatrice, June Bug, and Ramsay all stared at her.

"That's right. Her name is Laura. That's all I really know about her. I don't even have a last name for her. Anyway, she's apparently been making something of a pest of herself since her mother passed away. Apparently, she doesn't have a lot of money, which puts her in good company with the rest of Lester's family. All except for Archibald, I suppose. He seems to have money."

Shirley held out her hands. "That's all I know. So if I could leave now? I have some grocery shopping to take care of."

Ramsay asked for her address, which she gave in a scornful tone.

As soon as Shirley was gone, Ramsay said, "I should go speak with Archibald. It looks like the state police are heading this way to speak with you, June Bug."

June Bug's eyes welled up with tears again and Ramsay added quickly, "They're just going to try to get the details straight, that's all."

"I'll stay with you," said Beatrice in a comforting voice and June Bug nodded gratefully.

Fortunately, the questions were short and the policeman asking them seemed kind. After a few minutes, he told them that they were free to go.

Beatrice and June Bug didn't need telling twice. Soon June Bug was in Beatrice's car and Beatrice was driving out the long driveway.

Beatrice glanced over at June Bug to see how she was doing. She was extremely quiet, but that was normal for June Bug. "Would you like me to take you home? I was thinking maybe it would be nice for you to put your feet up for a little while before you headed back to the bakery."

June Bug gave Beatrice a solemn but perplexed look as if she really didn't know what putting her feet up was like. The little woman was nearly always in bustling, productive motion, so that could well be the case.

"Rowena had everything under control at the bakery," continued Beatrice. "I'm sure she wouldn't mind taking over for the rest of the day."

June Bug shook her head. "No, thanks. I should go back to the shop."

"Can I help you out? I can't bake and I'm not sure about using a cash register, but I can certainly deliver baked goods."

June Bug gave her a smile—the first she'd seen that day. "Thanks, Beatrice. I'll be okay. Good to keep busy today. I can get a ride later to get my car—I think I might be a little shaky to drive."

And so Beatrice took her back to the bakery. Beatrice had no doubt she'd soon be as busy as she liked, considering the number of customers she spotted lined up at the counter. She was about to head back home to have some coffee and read the paper when her phone rang.

"Piper?" she asked, frowning as she picked up the phone. It was an unusual time for her daughter to call her—it was one of Will's preschool days and Piper would ordinarily be working at the elementary school.

"Hi Mama. I'm not feeling one-hundred percent right now, so I thought I should leave school and head home."

"Oh no! What's wrong?"

Piper said, "Don't worry—it doesn't seem like anything really awful. Just sort of an overall 'sick' feeling. I'm probably running a fever, too. There have been a few things circulating around the school and I guess it was my turn to catch something. I was just wondering if you could pick up Will for me when preschool lets out. I'm going to try to take a nap and see if I feel any better then."

"Of course I can get him. But how about if I take him to my house and let him play for a while? There's no point in you trying to tend to Will while you're under the weather. You'll get better faster if you rest in bed."

This time there was a smile in Piper's voice when she spoke. "Once a mom, always a mom! Thanks; I'll take you up on that."

There was still plenty of time before preschool let out, so Beatrice headed back home to follow her original plan of coffee and the paper. Because, as lovely as her grandson was, there wasn't a lot of time to just sit around when he was over. After the newspaper, she picked up around the house and made a beef casserole for dinner and put it in the fridge to bake later just in case her day got completely hijacked. That being done, she felt very smug. It was always a good feeling to think ahead and avoid any obstacles that might come up. If she accomplished nothing else that day, she was in good shape.

Glancing at the clock, she saw it was 12:45 and time to head out to the preschool. It was located in the church, so she'd have a chance to pop in and say hi to Wyatt on the way out.

She loved picking up Will at preschool. He was in the one-year-old program there and always seemed to have a happy day when he went. The teacher had the little ones sitting in a circle and singing songs during pick-up time. It seemed to be a good tactic because there were rarely any tears from the group when one child was picked up earlier than another. Plus, the preschool wing was just such a happy place—the children's colorful art-work hung on the walls down the hall and there were cheerful banners hanging overhead. It was a comfy, fun spot.

Will looked briefly surprised to see his grandmother picking him up instead of his mother, but quickly toddled over for a hug, giving that cute, guttural name he had for Beatrice instead of "grandmama". He carefully took his tiny backpack off the hook in the hall and showed Beatrice a painting he'd made with sponges earlier that day.

"It's wonderful!" said Beatrice, looking at the painting. "Look at all the great colors you used. What's your favorite?"

Will's favorite color du jour (it did seem to change whenever Beatrice asked the question) was red. And indeed, red was the primary color used in the painting.

"Want to go see your granddad?" asked Beatrice.

Will's face brightened and he nodded. Beatrice guessed Wyatt was probably in his office eating lunch since it was now one o'clock. Fortunately, she was right. Wyatt was just finishing up his sandwich when they poked their heads in.

"Well, hi there! How are two of my most-favorite people?" asked Wyatt as Will bounded over to give him a hug and to show him his sponge painting.

"Wow, look at all that red!" said Wyatt, admiring the artwork.

Will beamed at him.

"How is everything going?" asked Wyatt. He had a vaguely puzzled expression on his face. "Somehow I was thinking that this was Piper's day to collect Will from school."

Beatrice glanced over at Will, but he'd happily taken a truck he'd brought for show-and-tell from his miniature backpack and was playing with it on the floor. "Piper isn't feeling too well right now so I offered. We're going to hang out at the house for a while and let her have the chance to get some sleep and see if she feels better afterward."

Wyatt nodded. "That makes sense."

Beatrice glanced at Will again, but he was still entranced with the truck and was making all sorts of truck sounds. "The morning was quite an adventure." She quickly filled him in on Lester's death and how June Bug had discovered him.

"Awful. I'm glad you let me know. I'll need to reach out to the family this afternoon. Archibald, in particular."

Archibald was so involved with the church that he had a lot of clout. Beatrice said, "I spoke to Archibald for a little while there. He was interested in knowing what your schedule was like for fitting in a service. I told him that your schedule could be easily changed, under the circumstances."

"Absolutely. How was the family holding up?"

"Well, I really just had the chance to speak with Archibald. I'll need to get in touch with Mellie, of course. Jack wasn't there and I didn't see Tilda."

Wyatt nodded. "It must have been a real shock to them, especially since it doesn't sound like it was a natural occurrence."

"Exactly. It makes things so much worse."

Wyatt said a little absently, "I need to call and let the bereavement committee know about Lester's death."

Beatrice smiled. "I'm sure the church ladies will jump into action. There will be casseroles in every oven this afternoon. Well, just wanted to fill you in real quick. I'd better get Will on home for a snack and let you make your phone calls."

"Is he still taking an afternoon nap, or is it going to be a lively afternoon for you?"

Beatrice chuckled. "The afternoon nap is probably a fifty-fifty shot. But the chances are better on days he has preschool, so fingers crossed."

They said goodbye to Wyatt and headed out.

Chapter Four

As they walked out to the car, Beatrice said to her grandson, "I thought we'd go to my house for a while and play. Does that sound good?"

It did to Will. But then, he had a special basket of toys in Beatrice's house that he only played with when he was visiting her. He was always happy to play either with Beatrice or by himself when he was there. Really, he was a most agreeable child, Beatrice decided.

When Beatrice was unloading Will at her house, Meadow, her next-door neighbor and co-grandmother, spotted them. She pulled right up into the driveway and hopped out of the car. "Is something wrong? This isn't supposed to be your day with Will!"

Will scampered over and hugged Meadow around a leg. Meadow stooped down and cuddled him, cooing at the boy as she did. "What a big boy you are! Did you have a good day at preschool?"

As Will filled Meadow in, Beatrice stifled a sigh. Meadow was sure to fly into high alert and swoop in trying to fix everything. "Piper called to say she was feeling under the weather.

She's at home resting now, so I picked up Will and am keeping him here for a while."

Meadow's eyes widened. "Under the weather? It's not the flu, is it? I've been hearing all sorts of horrid things on the news about it. It's a nasty one this year."

"She didn't sound that bad off. Let's keep our fingers crossed. Maybe it's just one of those twenty-four-hour bugs that circulates around elementary schools. A good nap might make her as right as rain."

Meadow was already scheming on how to fix the broken Piper. "I make an absolutely wonderful chicken noodle soup."

"I have no doubt about that." Meadow was an excellent cook. Her specialty was anything she set her mind to. Right now, that sounded like comfort food.

"I read an article on the healing power of chicken noodle soup. Did you know it really does have curative properties? I'll head right back home and whip up a big batch. And of course I'll give you a hand with Will this week. It would be my *pleasure*." Meadow gave Will another cuddle and the little guy laughed.

Beatrice gave her a weak smile. "Well, I'm sure Piper would love the soup. And Ash will, too."

Meadow frowned. "Ash will also need to step in to help. Piper might need some good nursing-type care."

"I think that's a little early to predict," protested Beatrice again.

But Meadow didn't seem to hear her. "He will also need to have a bigger role in doing the housework. The laundry will pile up if he's not careful."

Meadow had taken Piper's minor illness and blown it up to something catastrophic.

"Let's just play it all by ear. Except for your chicken noodle soup, which sounds lovely. Now Will and I are going to go have a snack and play for a little while before naptime."

At the mention of naptime, Will's little face fell. Beatrice gave an inward groan. Perhaps she shouldn't even have made a mention of it. At this point, she was thinking she might want to have some naptime, too.

Meadow frowned. "There was one other thing I wanted to ask you about. Now what was it?"

Beatrice shifted on her feet. She was ready to go in.

"Oh, *I* know. Ramsay took a call this morning and had to rush out of the house. He has been ignoring my phone calls so far which usually means something big has happened in town. Do you know anything about what might be going on?"

"Actually, I do," she admitted slowly. "June Bug called me to come pick her up. She was delivering a cake to Lester Dawson's house and she and Lester's housekeeper discovered his body."

Meadow's eyes grew huge again. "You're kidding."

Beatrice shook her head. "Apparently, it's a suspicious death."

"And you weren't going to mention this to me?" asked Meadow indignantly.

"After Piper called, everything else just sort of faded to the background."

Meadow considered this and then nodded. "I suppose I can see where that could happen. But this is a pretty big deal. Lester is a very important person in town and so is Archibald." Then she gasped. "And poor Mellie! Oh, I'll have to give her a call. No, I'll just plan on cooking for her and bringing it over. Not chicken noodle soup, though. Maybe a fried chicken platter with all the fixings. Comfort food of a different sort."

Beatrice saw this might be a good time to escape from Meadow. "I'd better head on inside," she said firmly.

Meadow gave her a vague look. "What? Oh, right. I should get to the store. I have some shopping to do." She wandered back to her car to further contemplate an appropriate meal for Mellie and her family and drove away.

Beatrice set out a nice snack for Will of fruit (cut up into bits) and graham crackers with peanut butter. He'd apparently worked up an appetite at preschool, despite being served lunch there because the food quickly disappeared. He gave Beatrice a grin. "Grmm."

Not quite "grandmama," but it warmed Beatrice's heart just the same. She gave him a cuddle. "Want to go play for a while?"

"Pleh!" he agreed.

While Will set about playing with the toys from the toy box, Beatrice cleaned up the kitchen before joining him. After a few minutes, her phone rang. She left Will happily playing with blocks and some plastic zoo animals.

"Piper? How are you feeling?"

"I wish I had a better report, but I feel pretty rotten. My head is killing me and I've got a temperature of 102."

Beatrice winced. "Honey, that sure sounds like the flu. Do you think you can get yourself to the doctor?"

Piper gave a light laugh. "Oh, Meadow's already offered."

Of course she had. Meadow had probably checked in on Piper as soon as she'd left Beatrice's house.

"I hope you're taking her up on the offer. You don't sound as if you need to be driving." Beatrice sometimes felt as if *Meadow* didn't need to be driving, but she was better than Piper in this situation.

"She's coming over in a few minutes to drive me over. I just wanted to give you an update. How's Will doing?"

Beatrice glanced over at Will who was delightedly building block towers only to knock them down immediately with great glee. "He's as happy as a clam. He had a good day at preschool, made a beautiful painting with sponges, said hi to Wyatt in his office, visited with Meadow, had a snack, and is now playing with blocks."

Piper chuckled. "You always give very detailed reports. I like that. When I ask Meadow how she's doing, she gushes about how smart or how cute he is. But you tell me what he's been *doing*."

"It's what I'd want in an update, myself! Look, I'm going to let you go, sweetie. Get ready to go to the doctor and then head back to bed. Meadow can fill me in later."

The next thirty minutes passed by very quietly with Will playing and her dog, Noo-noo, watching with interest. Then Beatrice started to notice that Will was rubbing his eyes quite a bit. She decided to approach the dangerous nap topic from a diplomatic standpoint.

"Will?" she asked.

Will looked at her with a smile. "Grrm?"

"Grandmama is feeling sleepy right now. I'm going to lie down and take a nap. Noo-noo is sleepy too. She wants to take a nap."

Noo-noo, unfortunately, perked up at the sound of her name and her bright brown eyes didn't seem sleepy in the slightest.

Will gave them both curious looks as if they were odd and interesting specimens indeed for wanting naps.

"How about if *Will* takes a nap, too?" This was Beatrice's grand finale.

Will considered this carefully before saying slowly, "No."

"No? How about if you just lie down and read a book for a little while?"

Will, of course, despite the genius status that Meadow had bestowed on him, wasn't yet able to read. But he loved looking at the pictures and knew the stories by heart. Sometimes Beatrice could hear him murmuring the words to himself as he turned the pages.

She had her fingers crossed. She really didn't want to return a fractious child to Ash and Piper when they were already dealing with other issues.

Will thought it through as Beatrice held her breath. "Okay," he finally said.

Beatrice tucked him into the tiny guest room of the cottage where she had a little toddler bed set up on the floor. She surrounded him with books and left one of the blinds partly open so he'd have enough light to see the pages. She also turned a small fan on, which made some lovely white noise.

Then she went into the living room again and picked up her own book. She'd lately been wanting to read some of her favorite comfort reads from her childhood again, so she'd picked *The Secret Garden*. She loved the transformation of Mary in the story and the mystery and the magic of the hidden garden that worked wonders in both Mary and Colin.

Noo-noo decided she perhaps *was* in the mood for a nap and soon the corgi was lying on her back with her short legs in the air and snoring lightly, giving little twitches from time to time.

Beatrice smiled at the sight. Noo-noo clearly didn't have very much stress in her life. If only her owner's life was so easy.

She tiptoed into the back bedroom to try and take an unobserved view of Will. As suspected, he was lightly snoring, and his books were scattered on him and beside him as he slept, his thumb tucked into his mouth.

Then it was Beatrice's turn. She stretched out on the sofa, throwing a small quilt over her legs. Soon, she joined Noo-noo and Will in the Land of Nod.

She was awakened sometime later by the sound of little feet running before Will happily launched himself at her.

"Well, hi there!" she said to him brightly.

"Grann!"

It was definitely a closer variation on the grandmama theme. "Let's see what time it is. Goodness, we slept forever. I'll have to tell you the story of Rip van Winkle and how long *his* nap was. It's a cautionary tale."

Will grinned his gummy grin at her.

A couple of hours had gone by, which was actually *not* ideal for either Beatrice nor Will. Both of them might end up being night owls that evening. She would have set an alarm for herself if she'd realized how tired the events of the day had made her. Will had clearly been exhausted from preschool and took a much-longer nap than expected, too.

And why hadn't anyone called her with an update on Piper?

Beatrice said, "Let's find out how Mama's doing."

She pulled out her phone, but before she could dial Ash or Meadow's number (she didn't want to wake up Piper if she was still sleeping), there was a knock at her door. Glancing outside, she said, "It looks like Granny has come for a visit."

Will ran over to join her as she opened the door. "Granny!" he said, articulating Meadow's grandmother name perfectly.

"How's the best grandchild ever?" asked Meadow as Will gave her a hug around her legs.

"Made picture!" Will bounded off to grab his sponge painting he'd made at preschool.

"Would you look at that?" said Meadow, studying the boy's artwork through her red bifocals. "A gorgeous painting! Look at your inspired use of color."

Will bounced back off to resume playing with his blocks and plastic animals. It appeared to Beatrice that zoo animals and farm animals appeared to be living together in peaceful harmony in Will's block world. The lion contentedly sat next to a cow.

Meadow said, "Best grandson ever."

"He is. But right now, I'm interested more in my best daughter ever. Have you heard any word from Piper? Didn't you take her to her doctor appointment?"

Meadow sighed. "It's flu, Beatrice. And she feels pretty rotten. But the doctor put her on an antiviral medicine and said she'd feel a bit better soon. It sounded like she'll mostly need rest.

"Thank heaven for that. Still, I'm sure she's miserable right now."

Meadow said, "I got her all fixed up with chicken noodle soup. The only problem is that she doesn't have any appetite right now. I tried to tempt her but she fell asleep right before I handed her a cup of it. Maybe she'll feel like having some after another nap. Going to the doctor took a lot out of her."

"I expect it did. Thank you, Meadow."

Meadow grinned at her. "It was my pleasure. Ash is knocking off early from the college since his classes are done for the day and is planning on looking after Piper for us. I'll keep Will for a while at my house since you've had him all afternoon."

"I loved every bit of it. Are you sure you'd like to bring him home?"

As soon as the words left her lips, she realized what a stupid question it was. Of *course* Meadow wanted to take Will home with her. She'd likely been looking forward to the opportunity all afternoon.

Meadow snorted. "I'll treasure every minute. While I was cooking for Piper and for Mellie, I went ahead and cooked for Ramsay and me, too. Will is going to have a feast! Maybe you and I can bring Mellie the food tomorrow."

Beatrice nodded, amazed at how productive Meadow had been. Cooking, caring for Piper, and a trip to the doctor? She clearly hadn't had a two-hour nap. Which reminded her that she should mention something about that to Meadow.

"Just a heads-up—Will and I had a nap this afternoon."

"Oh you *were* able to persuade him to lie down. How clever of you, Beatrice!"

Beatrice said wryly, "Yes, but the problem is that we slept for two hours instead of one. Far over our allotted time. I guess this morning must really have knocked me out."

"Naturally! We're not spring chickens, either one of us. It's distressing to have our days go off into unexpected and stressful tangents. I bet you're just as stressed from Piper being ill as you are from the unexpected events this morning. It must have been a nasty surprise after the morning you'd already had to get a call from Piper saying she was doing poorly."

That rang true. Beatrice said, "Have you heard any updates from Ramsay about the case? I was just wondering if he has any leads."

"I haven't heard a word. But I'll text him an adorable picture of Will and I have the feeling he'll at least swing by to eat supper at some point. I'm glad you filled me in, Beatrice. I swear, if I had to rely on Ramsay for information, I'd never know what's going on."

Beatrice helped pack up Will's things for Meadow and then waved as she and Will headed back over to Meadow's house.

Chapter Five

The next morning, Beatrice was up for good at four a.m. after a restless night's sleep. She showered and dressed, let out Noo-noo and fed her, and then settled down with the newspaper and some coffee. Then she even put some makeup on for good measure. She wondered how Piper was doing and how her night had been.

Wyatt woke up at a more-normal six o'clock. He looked a little confused at the sight of his wife completely ready for the day at such an early hour. "Everything okay?" he asked, rubbing his eyes and trying to focus. "Heard from Piper?"

"No, it was that mongo-nap I had yesterday afternoon. Apparently, my body thinks I've had enough sleep, even though I'm starting to feel like I could use some more." Beatrice sighed. "No word yet from Piper or Ash. Hopefully, everyone got some decent rest last night."

"Are you taking Will today?"

"I think I'd be babysitting over Meadow's dead body," said Beatrice dryly. "She sent me an email last night saying it was 'her day with Will.'"

"Would you like to go with me to visit the Dawson family, then? Archibald said he'd meet us over at Tilda's house."

Beatrice realized it was indeed Tilda's house now. She gave a little shiver. It was hard to imagine being alone and rattling around in that huge stone edifice. But maybe the house was full of good memories for Tilda that brought some comfort to her. Just because the house wasn't to Beatrice's liking didn't' mean it wasn't to Tilda's.

"Sure, I'd be happy to come along. Should we bring some food with us?"

Wyatt said, "I did call the church ladies after I spoke with you yesterday and they're heading over there this morning around nine. They've apparently got an arsenal of edibles."

Beatrice could only imagine. The church ladies were a rather formidable group of women. They mobilized with precision when members had deaths in the family, hospitalizations, and other life issues. Not only did they usually bring a lot of food for a variety of different meals, they also brought food to go in the freezer. You could survive solely on what they brought over for at least a month.

"So we're heading there after they arrive and unload, I'm guessing?" asked Beatrice.

Wyatt nodded. "Archibald said nine-thirty. I'm going to head over to the office first and get a little work done on my next sermon there. Then I can pick you up on the way out."

"Perfect," said Beatrice. Her phone rang and she looked at it. "Oh, it's Ash."

She picked up quickly and Ash said in a tired voice, "Everything's fine, Beatrice. I just wanted to give you a quick update before I take Will over to my mom and dad's house."

"Is Piper any better?"

Ash said, "Her fever's better, but she's really achy all over. She did manage to eat some of my mom's chicken noodle soup last night."

Beatrice chuckled. "Well, that's a relief. For one, she needed a little sustenance to fight off the flu. For another, Meadow would have hounded her at different intervals today until she had some."

"You've got that right! That was the first thing Mom asked me when I called her up to tell her I'm bringing Will over."

Beatrice said, "Do you think Piper needs anyone to look after her today? I've got some time this afternoon. Actually, my whole day can be reorganized, if need be." She didn't *need* to go to Tilda's house, after all. That was something Wyatt could handle if he needed to.

"Honestly, I think it would be better if she just slept today. She'll probably feel a ton better just getting a little rest. And, if she's sleeping, she won't need anyone waiting on her."

Beatrice asked with a little trepidation, "How did *Will* sleep last night?"

Ash snorted. "Sleep? Will played all night in his bed. I woke up at two and could hear him talking to himself.

Beatrice felt a little pang of guilt. No wonder Ash sounded so tired. "Sorry about that. He and I had quite a nap yesterday."

"Oh, it's okay. I wasn't going to sleep anyway because I'd moved over to the sofa in the hopes of avoiding getting the flu, myself. I guess I haven't tried sleeping on a sofa for a while because it didn't work out too well. My neck is killing me."

"Hope you can catch up on your sleep tonight."

"Maybe. Well, I'd better head out for work, Beatrice. Thanks for looking after Will yesterday."

Beatrice said, "It was my pleasure. Every minute of it." She hung up and updated Wyatt.

"So we're still on for going to see Tilda?" he asked.

"Sounds good. Ash said that Piper just needed to sleep today."

Wyatt headed off to the church office while Beatrice did a little housework and then surveyed the cottage to see if anything else needed to be done. She grimaced when she spotted two sad-looking houseplants. Although Beatrice somehow had rotten luck with growing things indoors, she kept trying because she *wanted* living things inside with her. She just didn't understand how she could be so successful with her shrubs and flowerbeds outdoors but couldn't seem to keep things alive in the house.

She picked up the plants and moved them out of the sunbeam they were in and then watered them generously. But as she did, she wondered if she should be giving them *more* light and *less* water. Maybe she was just making the situation worse. She'd have to ask someone at the garden center about it.

After vacuuming and filling up the birdfeeders in the backyard, Beatrice headed back in to quickly comb her hair and touch up her makeup. She finished just in time for Wyatt's arrival at the house.

In the car on the way over, Beatrice asked, "What do you know about Tilda Dawson? I don't know her well at all. Actually, I didn't really know Lester, either."

Wyatt nodded. "Both of them tended to keep to themselves, I think, and stayed at home most of the time. I guess they preferred it that way. Their children seem to be a lot more outgoing. You're friends with Mellie, I think?"

"She's a quilting friend of mine, so I see her mainly at quilt shows or at Posy's shop. But we've seen the odd movie together, you remember."

Wyatt said slowly, "Oh, that's right. She's a fan of costume dramas, isn't she?" He gave Beatrice an apologetic look. "I should try a little harder to be more interested in them."

"If you're not a fan, you're not a fan. There's no point in trying to force something. Besides, movies are too expensive to sleep through." She gave him a teasing look. The last time he'd accompanied her to a film set in the 1700s, he'd been gently snoring a third of the way through.

"I'm glad you've got a friend to see them with. It's got to be more fun going with someone who's actually excited to be there." He paused. "I'm sorry . . . there was a question you'd asked and I've forgotten it."

"About Tilda. What she's like."

"Oh, right. I'm not sure I know her any better than you do, unfortunately. I've run into her at the church a few times, but she's not regularly in the pews. She's very elegant, but you'd know that from the times you've seen her."

Beatrice said, "Yes, that's about my only impression of her. The times I've run into her have been at the store. She's always stopped and asked how you were doing. She'd say she intended on going to a church service soon. But I never got the impression she was very happy, somehow. Her smile never seemed to get all the way to her eyes."

"I've had the same impression. I hoped I was misreading her. That maybe she was just reserved."

Wyatt pulled the car in front of the Dawson home and they got out of the car. It looked like a couple of the church ladies were just leaving. One of them, a stolid, grim woman, came over to give a quick report.

"We've got her all set up with food for a while." She carefully detailed the breakfast and supper casseroles for the fridge and freezer, the selection of various sandwiches for lunch (all with the crusts cut off), and the gallon of sweet tea and paper plates and cups they'd dropped off to help them cut down on washing dishes.

"Thank you all so much," said Wyatt. "I'm sure the family really appreciates it."

A smile hovered around the church lady's mouth, but she didn't allow it to fully blossom. "We've already been to Archibald's with food for him." She paused and said, "His wife is apparently not living there right now."

"I'm sorry to hear that," said Wyatt.

The church lady looked as if she'd like to delve further into the subject but then pressed her lips together as if realizing perhaps the best person to gossip with wasn't her minister. "We asked Tilda if we could bring food to Mellie and Jack, but she said they'd be coming by the house later and she would distribute some of the casseroles to them."

"That sounds perfect. Thank you, Betty."

Betty bobbed her head and strode off.

Wyatt rang the doorbell and Imelda, the housekeeper, answered it. The woman's face was pale and puffy, as if from crying, lack of sleep, or both. Wyatt said gently, "Good morning. Beatrice and I are here to speak with Tilda about service arrangements."

The housekeeper said, "Please follow me."

They did, walking through a tremendous three-story foyer into a large living room. The walls of the room were wainscoted and covered with old tapestries depicting hunting scenes. The floors were a dark wood and the furniture was all Victorian antique. The overall effect was rather chilly, thought Beatrice, pulling her light sweater farther around her.

Tilda rose to greet them. As Wyatt and Beatrice had been discussing, she was wearing elegant, tailored clothes. The lines on her face were standing out in sharp relief as if she hadn't slept well the previous night.

"It's so good of you both to come by," she said in a rote fashion, gesturing to an antique sofa. "Won't you sit down?"

Wyatt and Beatrice perched on it. Tilda seemed oddly absent, as if she really was only half paying attention to her guests. What's more, the expression on her face made Beatrice wonder if she was perhaps taking some sort of prescription to calm her nerves a little.

"We're very sorry about Lester," said Wyatt. "What a horrible shock it must have been."

Tilda nodded. "It was. I slept in yesterday because I'd had a headache and had no idea what happened until Imelda came to get me after she'd called the police." She gave a shiver. "I decided not to go into his office. I didn't want to remember him like that. And to have it happen on his birthday, of all times." A tear slid down her cheek.

"Such awful timing," murmured Beatrice. Although, of course, there never was a good time to lose someone.

Tilda said, "I've been thinking back to when I first started dating Lester all those years ago. I was still a kid, really. Lester was older, of course, and was so focused and had so much direction and promise. And energy. I was drawn to all that energy of his. Our marriage wasn't perfect. How many are? But there was so much to admire about Lester."

"He certainly seemed to have a lot of drive. And I know he cared deeply for his family," said Wyatt.

Beatrice thought she saw a hint of doubt on Tilda's features before it was quickly replaced. "Of course," she said coolly.

Wyatt said, "Is Archibald here? I know he was interested in discussing the funeral arrangements."

Tilda sighed and reached over to a single sheet of paper that was lying on a nearby mahogany table. "He's not here right now, but he's already made his decision on the arrangements. He typed them up and left them here for you."

Wyatt stood to take the paper from her and glanced over it as he sat again. He hesitated. "Are these plans all right with you, Tilda?"

Tilda shrugged a thin shoulder. "He cares more than I do about the service, so we'll go with his ideas."

"Did Lester ever discuss his plans for a service with you?" asked Beatrice.

This made Tilda smile. "No, that's not the kind of conversation we would have had with each other. I believe part of Lester thought he might be able to defeat death if he put his mind to it. He's always been able to do anything he wanted to do. He did end up living for a very long time, didn't he? Anyway, Lester and I didn't get into very deep discussions. We led fairly separate lives and kept out of each other's way to a certain extent. Sometimes marriages operate better that way, don't you think?"

Wyatt and Beatrice obediently nodded although neither felt that way.

"We always did have one meal a day with each other. Sometimes one of our children would join us," she said.

"It's nice for you to have your family so close, especially during such a difficult time," said Wyatt.

"Yes. I'm very proud of our children." Tilda said it in a rote manner, almost as if it was something she said so often that it had become automatic. "Mellie is really coming into her own now. Beatrice, you know Mellie, don't you?"

"I do—we're quilting friends."

Tilda said, "Did you know she's started an online business?"

"No, I didn't. Is it quilting-related?" asked Beatrice.

Tilda shrugged again. "You'd have to ask her, I'm afraid. I think so, but I didn't completely follow what she was talking about. Mellie will be such a big help clearing the house."

Wyatt asked, "Are you planning on moving?"

"Oh, no, I don't think so. I've spent too many years here and have too many memories to ever consider leaving. But I'd like the interior of the house to be more to my taste. Everything in here was pretty much procured by Lester." She glanced over at Beatrice again. "Aren't you an art curator?"

"I was before I retired, yes. With an emphasis on Southern folk art."

Which was clearly not in evidence here in the Dawson mansion. The walls were full of rather grim portraiture of illustrious forebears. The other paintings she saw seemed to be mainly landscapes.

Tilda glanced around her. "I'd just like to see the place brightened up a little. Modernized. Bright colors and new furniture that's a bit more comfortable than what I have now. She gestured to the antique sofa where Wyatt and Beatrice were stiffly sitting.

"I'm sure Mellie will be a big help," said Beatrice.

"Let's just say it's something I can actually see her doing," said Tilda with a tight smile. "Archibald is always busy doing something or another to give me a hand. And Jack?" She waved her hands in the air to indicate the ephemeral nature of Jack's schedule. "But Jack is coming over in a little while to 'cheer me up,' he said." The tight smile turned into a genuine one.

Wyatt said, "That'll be nice."

"It will be. I can use something of a stress break. To be honest, I feel strangely drained."

Beatrice wondered if it was just exhaustion that had made Tilda seem so unfocused earlier. She probably didn't get much sleep the night before. Beatrice gave a small shudder at the thought of trying to sleep there. It was a very cold, rather sterile place. There weren't any family photos around, for one, nor any bright colors to offset the dark brown furniture and the stone walls. And it was incredibly quiet, aside from some far-away droning sounds of Imelda, vacuuming. With the unsettling death yesterday, it would be a rather creepy home to try and get some rest in.

There was a light tap on the front door and then Archibald abruptly entered. "Good morning," he called out. "Good to see you, Wyatt and Beatrice. Mother, you too."

Tilda gave him a chilly smile.

"Wyatt, I was wondering if I could speak with you for a few minutes," continued Archibald, clearly intending for it to be a private conversation.

Wyatt picked up the printed instructions for Lester's service. "Of course." He walked over to Archibald and they disappeared into another room.

Tilda gazed after them and then turned to Beatrice. "I'm sorry I didn't see you yesterday morning. The police allowed me to stay inside the house in a separate wing while they investigated." She paused. "I suppose you saw that woman when you were here."

"Woman?"

"Yes. What's-her-name. Shirley, I think."

Beatrice said, "Yes, we did see her at the house yesterday morning."

Tilda shook her head, looking blankly out the window. "Her coming over here was never part of the agreement."

Beatrice hesitated, not sure exactly how she was supposed to address the subject of Lester's other woman. She made a non-committal humming sound meant to convey empathy.

Tilda seemed encouraged to go on. "I didn't want to say anything in front of the minister, of course, but this arrangement that Lester had with her is no longer appropriate. Lester was paying that woman's mortgage. I feel no obligation to continue doing so. And now she seems to want to contact me." She frowned. "I suppose you know about this."

Beatrice said carefully, "Not very much. But I'm sure it must have been very difficult for you."

Tilda seemed surprised by this statement, but didn't say anything. "Well, it's certainly difficult now, that's for sure. She seems to think she has some sort of rights here because of her involvement with Lester. But she doesn't have any at all." An air of bleakness settled over her again.

"Have you spoken to Ramsay about it? I mean, if she's trespassing, as you're seeming to indicate."

Tilda considered this. "That might be a possibility. At least I could *threaten* her with calling Ramsay, at any rate. She's becoming something of a nuisance." She paused. "She keeps saying that Lester changed his will and left her a great deal of the estate."

"Does that sound like something Lester would have done?" Beatrice noticed Tilda's eyes drooping a little and reverted back to her original assessment. She definitely seemed medicated instead of merely sleepy. Perhaps that had something to do with the fact that she was telling Beatrice all of this highly-personal information.

"It certainly *doesn't* sound like something he'd have done. The little cottage he provided her was one thing. But this place," she waved her hand around airily again to indicate her home, "is something else. And think about it—it sure sounds like a motive for killing Lester, doesn't it? If that woman thought she was going to inherit Lester's estate? It's not as if she has very much money. She probably thought it would be the easiest way to get some."

Beatrice made that noncommittal sound again, which Tilda obviously considered encouragement. Tilda continued, "There may also have been a time factor involved. Lester rarely spoke about the woman, but he did say Shirley was becoming something of a nuisance and that he was planning on ending the relationship. I told Lester it had nothing to do with me, one way or another."

Beatrice said, "Did you tell Ramsay this? This might be very important for him to know."

Tilda shook her head. "I was in shock yesterday. I don't think Ramsay even knew about Shirley when he was speaking to me. I'm not sure what all I told him yesterday because it was mostly a blur, but I *know* I didn't speak with him about her." She looked over at Beatrice and gave a short laugh. "Sorry, you look sort of shocked."

"Oh, no," said Beatrice, although she sort of was. "Everyone is different, aren't they? Everyone's *marriage* is different."

"Very diplomatic of you. And that's very true. Our marriage, different as it was, worked well for *us*." Tilda's voice was just a bit slurred, which might explain why she was divulging so much information.

Archibald abruptly came back in just in time to hear his mother's slurred speech. He frowned, his gaze sharpening and his eyebrows knitting together. "Mother, isn't it time you went upstairs to rest for a while?"

Beatrice and Wyatt took that as a cue to leave. "Please let us know if there's anything Beatrice and I, or the church, can do," said Wyatt.

"Thank you," said Tilda, looking away.

Chapter Six

As Archibald walked them out, Beatrice added, "The ladies from the church came by with a good deal of food, I believe. You may want to take some things home with you."

"I appreciate that," said Archibald with a grim smile. "Very helpful."

The door closed behind them and Beatrice and Wyatt glanced at each other.

"It's a stressful time," murmured Wyatt as they walked to the car.

"Indeed it is," said Beatrice.

Wyatt started up the car and they rode away. Beatrice said, "Was it just me, or did Tilda seem a little off?"

"I think the doctor must have prescribed some medications for her to manage the stress." He glanced over at her. "How did you think she was?"

"I think she was definitely under the influence of something, but I can't really blame her, under the circumstances." Beatrice paused. "She didn't want to speak about it with you in the room, but she was telling me about the whole Shirley Keller thing."

"The Shirley . . . oh, that's right. You were telling me about that last night. Her relationship with Lester."

"Illicit relationship with Lester," said Beatrice dryly. "I advised her to tell Ramsay about some issues she's been having with Shirley. Apparently, Shirley's been hanging around on the property and claiming that Lester made provisions for her in his will."

Wyatt winced. "I can't imagine *that* went down well."

"No. But Tilda pointed out that it does make for a good motive for murder if Shirley believed she was inheriting some of Lester's estate."

Wyatt said, "Maybe it would be good for you to give Ramsay a call to let him know. Your conversation wasn't confidential as mine would have been with Tilda."

Beatrice frowned. "Speaking of confidential, Archibald seemed to be acting very secretive."

"He was discussing the service and wanted his mother kept out of the process," said Wyatt slowly. "I suppose he thought the discussion might upset her."

Beatrice snorted. "You're being far too generous. He probably believed she was going to try to make changes if she heard them discussed. Although I don't know why he worried, considering she basically handed us his outline for the service without saying a word."

Wyatt gave a little sigh. "Well, I can say I've heard complaints in the past about Archibald's management style at the church, so it doesn't come as a huge surprise that he's secretive. I understand he's one of those people who completely takes over a committee and does all the work himself. On the one hand, he's incredibly effective and efficient and always gets the job done. On the other, he tends to step on some toes along the way."

Wyatt pulled up into their driveway. "I'm going to head over to the church for a couple of meetings. What are your plans for the rest of the morning?"

"Checking in on Piper," said Beatrice promptly. "Once a mother, always a mother."

After Wyatt left, Beatrice put Noo-noo's harness on her and they went off for a walk. Beatrice dialed Piper as they went.

She picked up, sounding like she'd just woken up. "Mama?"

"Hey there, sweetie. Sorry for waking you up. I just wanted to see how you were doing."

Piper said, "You didn't wake me up—I was already stirring. I probably sound like I'm at death's door, but I'm actually feeling a lot better. The aches and pains are mostly gone, but I've still got enough fever to make me really sleepy. I'm just really lethargic."

"Of course you are. Flu is a terrible thing. Is your appetite back at all?"

Piper chuckled. "Well, I've been eating Meadow's chicken noodle soup, so that's something."

"I thought you ate that yesterday."

"Oh, she brought a vat of it," said Piper wryly.

"Yes, that sounds like Meadow. I'm going to let you go back to sleep now. Get some rest and I'll talk with you later."

She'd just hung up when her phone started ringing again. She picked it up, figuring Piper had forgotten to tell her something. "Yes?"

It was Meadow, though, and she sounded too frazzled to have absorbed Beatrice's unusual greeting. "I'm just so annoyed!"

"Is everything okay with Will?" asked Beatrice.

"Will is absolutely perfect, as always. But I have an eye doctor appointment this morning and I've tried to reschedule it. The doctor is completely booked up, though. Nothing is going according to schedule!"

Beatrice said in a calm voice that had worked well in settling Meadow down in the past, "Everything will be fine. You should go to your appointment. I'd be delighted to take Will. I've wanted to run by the Patchwork Cottage to pick up some fabric, anyway. He and I can go see Maisie."

Maisie was the chubby white cat that resided mainly at the quilt shop. She also spent time with Miss Sissy, a quilt shop regular and local eccentric.

"If you're sure," said Meadow. Her voice was very reluctant. It was clear she would much rather be spending the remainder of her morning with her grandson instead of at the eye doctor.

"Of course I am. I'll see you in a few minutes."

Beatrice turned them around to head back to the cottage and Noo-noo looked at her with a confused expression on her face.

"Sorry, Noo-noo. I know that wasn't much of a walk, was it, girl? Maybe you and I can take Will on a walk later."

They'd barely made it back to the house when Meadow pulled into the driveway. Will, in his car seat, was looking out the window and waving to Beatrice with a big smile on his face.

Meadow hopped out and opened the trunk of her car. "Such a morning!"

Beatrice helped her pull out Will's diaper bag and other assorted paraphernalia. She said, "Don't worry about the stroller. If Will and I go for a walk, I'll just hold his hand and skip the stroller."

"Sounds good. The appointment shouldn't take very long. Have you spoken to Piper lately?"

Beatrice filled her in and Meadow said, "That all sounds very promising. Especially that she's eating the soup! Maybe I should make some other meals for her. I have a boiled custard recipe that's to die for. And it's full of protein."

Beatrice could tell that Meadow was all-in on cooking. "I'm sure she'll love it."

"I can also bring some by to Miss Sissy. And I need to stuff some food down Ramsay's throat the next time he surfaces." Meadow frowned, thinking of her husband.

"Has he given you any updates on the investigation?"

Meadow snorted. "As if he would. He's been keeping it all under his hat. But he sure has been away from the house a lot. All right, well, I suppose I'd better head on to this blasted appointment."

"Just call me before you come over to the house. I might be out with Will."

"Will do."

Beatrice lifted Will out of Meadow's backseat and gave him a big hug. Will waved to Meadow as she drove away.

"Let's put Noo-noo in the house and then we'll run by to see Maisie at the shop. Do you need to have a snack before we go?"

Will thought about it with serious consideration and then shook his head. Beatrice wasn't surprised. If there was one thing Meadow excelled at, it was feeding people. Who knows how much food she'd plied their mutual grandson with?

So they let Noo-noo back in the house and set out for the Patchwork Cottage, hand in hand. The quilt shop was a bright, sunny, happy place that always lifted Beatrice's spirits as soon as she walked in. There were gingham curtains fluttering in the windows, lots of light beaming in, and Posy always had local musicians' music playing on the speaker. Plus, you were surrounded by quilts when you entered the shop, which lent a very cozy feel to the space.

Posy brightened when they walked in. "Well, hi, you two! What a pleasant surprise."

"We thought we'd run by and say hi, didn't we, Will?"

Will beamed at Posy and Posy stooped down on his level and said, "Guess what I have in the sitting area? I picked up some toys. They're in a little basket over by the sofa. And Maisie is back there, too, so you can say hi to her."

Will trotted off and Beatrice could hear cheerful greetings across the room. Posy smiled. "Savannah and Tiggy are playing Scrabble over there. I have the feeling they're glad to see Will."

Beatrice glanced over toward the back of the shop and said, "Wow, and Dan is here, too. A busy day for the Patchwork Cottage."

Dan was dating Tiggy, Savannah and Georgia's aunt. He gave Beatrice a wave when he heard his name.

Posy chuckled. "Always something else to fix here. We've got some leaky plumbing happening and Dan is on top of that." She paused and said, "I meant to get in touch with you yesterday after you got that call from June Bug. I heard what happened—Meadow phoned me."

Of course she had. Meadow had likely called quite a few people. It was for this very reason that Ramsay didn't divulge much information to her about his investigations.

Beatrice said, "June Bug was pretty shaken up, but seemed better by the time I dropped her back off at the bakery. Wyatt met with the family this morning to plan the service."

Posy shook her head. "It must have been a terrible shock to Mellie. I didn't see her here yesterday, of course. I'm sure she must have spent the day trying to take it all in."

"Has Mellie been spending more time than usual over here?"

"She sure has. She's starting up a quilting business online. I don't know all the details, but she's been over at the shop collecting fabrics and whatnot. I know she's making custom quilts for people."

Beatrice said, "That sounds like it might be a good business for her. I'm planning on running by some food for her with Meadow later, although she probably could get enough from her mom's house to feed an army."

Posy smiled, her blue eyes twinkling. "Did the church ladies strike again?"

"They did indeed."

Beatrice glanced over to quickly check on Will, but he was happily playing some sort of make-believe game involving sports cars and a castle.

There was a sound of a large truck engine and then a beeping noise indicating the truck was backing up. Posy's eyes opened wide. "Oh, mercy. I bet that's my fabric delivery."

"Shouldn't that be a good thing?"

"Usually it is," said Posy slowly, "but our deliveryman is Jack Dawson."

Lester's youngest child. Beatrice said, "Maybe there's a substitute driver today. Surely there must be."

But there wasn't. Posy held the door open wide as a handsome blond man in his late-thirties came in with a large box.

"Hi there, Posy," he said cheerfully. "I've got a few deliveries for you."

Posy stumbled over her words, finally saying, "Goodness, Jack. I'm so sorry you're having to worry about this today. I heard the terrible news about your father."

Jack looked more solemn. "Yes. It was a real shock for the family."

There was an awkward silence for a few seconds before Will toddled back over to take a look at the newcomer.

Jack beamed at him. "Well, hi there. Have you got yourself a car?"

Will nodded, giving him a grin that showed off his new teeth. "I pleh."

Beatrice was ready to translate for Jack, but he seemed to fully understand that Will meant "play."

"Do you like cars and trucks, then?"

Will nodded again, very enthusiastically.

"Want to go check out my delivery truck?" Jack asked. He gave Beatrice a quick questioning look and she gave a nod.

Will's eyes grew big and Beatrice held his hand as they walked outside the shop to explore the truck. Jack certainly seemed in no hurry to finish delivering Posy's packages or heading on to the next stop, but Will loved every second of his tour. Jack let him get into the driver's seat and Will started making truck sounds as he turned the steering wheel. Then he accidentally honked the horn, which made Will give a delighted gurgling laugh. Jack laughed too, but Beatrice winced as an old lady jumped in the street, glaring at Jack as if it were all his fault.

While Will continued pretending he was driving the truck, Jack said, "My mom said you and Wyatt stopped by for a visit this morning. How did she seem to you? I'm heading over there after work."

Beatrice thought again about how spacy Tilda had seemed. She didn't think it was her place to say anything, though, especially since Jack would see that for himself, later. She said, "She was very calm and measured. Sad, of course, but handling it well."

Jack said, "Well, that definitely sounds like Mom! She's always very controlled with her emotions." He paused. "Actually, I guess Archibald is probably the same way. Lester was, too, although he at least showed anger sometimes. That was the one emotion he didn't freeze out."

Beatrice noticed Jack called his father "Lester." She wondered if that was just Jack being casual or if it indicated something about the relationship between Lester and his son.

Will made more truck noises and Jack laughed. Then he gave Beatrice a wry look. "Sorry about the levity. It might seem inappropriate in light of Lester's death. And I *am* sorry about his passing—only because it's giving my mother added stress. But the fact of the matter is that my father was a miserable man. He was miserable to deal with and miserable *inside* of himself. He wasn't happy and he spread that unhappiness to anyone in his path. I kept out of his way as much as I could so his bitterness didn't affect me, too."

Beatrice nodded. "Sometimes it's best that way."

Jack gave her an appreciative smile. "It is, although it's unfortunate. What I felt for Lester was pity. I felt sorry for him for years. He had everything—money and family—but couldn't seem to find happiness. He was like a lost soul in the desert."

Beatrice must have looked a little surprised by his poetic bent because Jack laughed. "Ramsay and I are in a poetry and writing group together. I'm not sure I'm any good at it, but it's a nice hobby to have. It's cheap and it helps me keep my head together. Well, as much as I'm able to," he added wryly.

"Ramsay must be interesting to have in your group. He and I have sort of an unofficial book club. He recommends reads for me and I recommend them for him. Sometimes we like each other's picks and sometimes not."

Jack chuckled. "I bet. I have the feeling Ramsay's taste in literature runs to the grim and inscrutable. You're right, though—he's great to have in our group. He's a very dedicated writer. The only bad thing is now he's been put in the position of thinking of me as a suspect."

Beatrice had wondered if that was going to come up. "That must be awkward for you both."

"It's mostly just awkward for Ramsay. I totally understand that he has to do his job. If there's one thing I understand, it's work. I make a pretty decent suspect, I guess. I have absolutely no alibi since I was at home by myself. Plus, it's pretty obvious that I wasn't the biggest fan of Lester's." He shrugged. "Plus, I always need money. All that stuff sort of adds up to make me look like I might be guilty."

"It must have been tough not having a close tie with your father, but it sounds like you're close with your mom. She's looking forward to seeing you later today. It sounds like the two of you have a great relationship."

Jack's face softened a little as he thought of his mother. "We do. I've always tried to get Mom out of that miserable pile of bricks as often as possible. We'd meet out for lunch or coffees. I think it was good for her to get away from the poisonous atmosphere inside that house. Not only is the place too dark, but Lester didn't help make it more cheerful."

"That's very good of you to take your mom out. I'm sure Tilda must have appreciated that."

Jack had a faraway look in his eyes. "Mom told me she slipped into the room to see Lester, you know. Before the police came."

That wasn't what Tilda had said, Beatrice noted. She'd said she'd stayed out of there because she didn't want to see what had happened to Lester. But then, perhaps she didn't want to talk about what she'd seen or relive it. Except with Jack.

"Do you know what the murder weapon was?" asked Jack.

Beatrice shook her head.

"His briefcase. Isn't that ironic? He had that thing with him all the time, like his armor. It was packed full of spite, pique, and information that his private investigators got for him." Jack pressed his lips together as if he'd said too much. "Let's just say it was heavy. Clearly it was, if it could be used to kill him."

Beatrice was quiet for a moment, digesting this information, and Jack continued, "It must sound like I hated Lester. I really didn't. I don't hold anything against him except for the way he treated Mom. But I've had to face the fact that she did make a choice. She was the one who decided to throw her life away with Lester and not escape."

"Maybe the marriage had its happy moments, too?" suggested Beatrice.

Jack gave a short laugh. "You're clearly an optimist. But then, you're married to a minister, aren't you? It probably comes with the territory." He paused. "There were times when Mom was content, I'm sure of that. I think she felt she'd invested too much time in the marriage to leave Lester. She didn't want it all to be wasted time."

Beatrice said, "Do you have any thoughts about what might have happened to Lester? Who might be behind all this?"

"Well, the only thing I can tell you for sure is that Mom didn't have anything to do with it. My mother cared about my dad in her way and she would never have even thought about harming him. It could easily have been somebody from outside the family—that house wasn't exactly Fort Knox. The doors are always unlocked because there are service staff coming in and out all the time. Lester made plenty of people upset with him, so I'm sure it could be an outsider. Who knows—maybe he even made some of the staff angry enough to take a swing at him? I will say there's one particular person who stands out, though. Laura Ellis. Have you heard about her?"

Will put his chubby hands on the horn again while he looked questioningly at his grandmother. Beatrice shook her head at him. He gave a small sigh and contented himself with making more truck sounds as he turned the steering wheel.

"I believe I might have," admitted Beatrice.

"No surprise, considering it's a small town. Anyway, she's Lester's illegitimate daughter—at least, according to her. I guess we don't have any actual proof of that claim. She's here in town and she'd been harassing Lester by phone and in person. Don't get me wrong, I do have a lot of sympathy for her, if she's telling the truth, and I totally understand the position she's in. But she's also very obviously full of anger and a sense of being wronged."

Beatrice nodded.

Jack continued, "She didn't grow up with any of the advantages that she should have as one of Lester's children. We had swimming lessons, horseback, camp, tutoring, golf, tennis, football. Of *course* she's angry—why wouldn't she be? But there's no reason for her to be here in town. She could have tried to communicate with Lester long-distance. You have to wonder why she showed up here in Dappled Hills."

Beatrice thought maybe Laura *had* tried to reach Lester long-distance and he hadn't been very welcoming. Perhaps that's why she'd shown up in person. Beatrice said slowly, "Does your mom know? About Laura, I mean?"

Jack nodded. "I'm sure Tilda was hurt when she found out—even if she didn't show it. But she's so used to Lester disappointing her that I think she was just generally numb whenever he'd behaved badly. Maybe she almost expected it. If you expect bad things to happen then you don't have to live with disappointment when they *do* happen. The thing that bothers me most about Lester's treatment of my mother is it made her sort of empty out her emotions as a defensive move. She didn't want to get hurt, so she tried not to care too much about anything."

"When the two of you went out for your lunches, did she open up more? Was she more like her usual self?"

Jack smiled. "She was sometimes. I loved seeing that glimpse of the old Mom. When I was a kid, she was still her natural self. Maybe, now that Lester's gone, she can be that way again. I really hope so. But now she's got to deal with all this craziness with Laura. Oh, and Shirley Keller, of course." He rolled his eyes. "Gossip being what it is, I'm sure you've heard of her, too."

"Actually, I didn't know anything about that until Archibald filled me in."

Jack raised his eyebrows. "Old Archie told you? That's surprising."

"It was more of him explaining who she was and why she was at the house yesterday morning when I was there."

"Ah. That makes sense. Well, I'm sure he was very annoyed to see Shirley over there at the house. The agreement between Lester and Shirley was that she was supposed to stay away from there, especially since she had her own place. The fact she was there at the house at all is very suspicious on its own. Maybe I shouldn't have thrown Laura under a bus. Maybe *Shirley* is the one responsible for all this."

Beatrice said, "She said she was on the grounds to check on your father when he didn't show up that morning."

"Convenient excuse. Whatever. She's an opportunist, obviously. What Shirley is getting wrong, though, is the idea that her relationship with Lester entitles her to anything else. My mother put in the time and heartache and she deserves the inheritance that's coming to her." He glanced at his watch and sighed. "Thanks for letting me rant about this stuff. Unlike most of my family, I don't really like to keep things bottled up inside. But I've gotta run now. These packages aren't going to deliver themselves."

He scooped up Will, swinging him up and down outside the truck as Will squealed with joy. "Maybe you can drive my truck another time, little man. You probably did a better job than I do. Let's deliver a couple more boxes to the shop, okay?"

Jack put Will down and Beatrice held the toddler's hand as Jack pulled out more deliveries for Posy. They brought them in and then Jack took off, blowing the truck horn one more time, to Will's delight. Will waved excitedly to Jack as he drove away.

Chapter Seven

Posy started unpacking the boxes and going through the contents. She smiled at Beatrice. "It sounds like Will was having fun out there."

"Oh, he was having the time of his life. Jack was nice to let him sit in the driver's seat and play make-believe." She paused. "I guess Meadow got held up at the ophthalmologist because she's taking longer than I thought she would. Maybe I should take Will over for a walk to the park."

Posy chuckled. "You'd better take Miss Sissy with you. She woke up from a nap and was irritated that no one had told her Will was here."

"I didn't even know she was back there! She could have come out while we were with the truck."

Posy shook her head. "All the honking was annoying her."

"I'll go make amends," said Beatrice. She looked down at Will, who was still holding her hand. "Do you want to say bye to Savannah and Tiggy? And Maisie, too? Maybe we can go to the park with Miss Sissy."

Will happily broke free and toddled over to the sitting area. He gently petted Maisie who rolled over on her back and gave him a feline smile. Will knew from experience that no matter how tempting Maisie's tummy might look, he needed to only scratch her sweetly under her chin.

Savannah and Tiggy looked up from their Scrabble game. "Hi there, Beatrice," said Tiggy. "How are things?"

"Oh, they're pretty good. I guess they're *always* good when I'm with Will. How's the game going?" Beatrice peered over at the board. "My goodness. *Quixotic*? *Wheezily*? This is next-level Scrabble."

Savannah preened. "Quixotic was mine. But then Aunt Tiggy came up with wheezily, so I guess we're probably even again."

Tiggy waved a tile at her and then carefully made *chutzpah* on the board.

Savannah gawped at the board and then sighed. "I think I'm going to have to think about my tiles more carefully. Beatrice, are you any good at this game?"

Beatrice shook her head. "Sadly, no. I have a decent vocabulary, but I have spatial processing issues. I can't seem to juggle letters around in my mind very well."

"I'm starting to think that I can't, either." Savannah tilted her head and peered at her letters as if the slight change of perspective might help.

Miss Sissy had fallen back asleep and was snoring along with the music Posy had playing quietly over the sound system. It was quite disconcerting to Beatrice. She walked over and gently put an arm on the old woman's shoulder. Miss Sissy continued snoring. Then Beatrice shook her shoulder a bit. Miss Sissy took a gasping, snorting breath and jerked her head up, making more wiry hair fall out of her bun and startling Beatrice in the process.

The old woman growled at Beatrice. Beatrice ignored her bad humor and said, "Would you like to walk to the park with Will and me? He'd like to play on the playground there."

Miss Sissy looked around to see Will and then smiled when she saw him on the floor still rubbing Maisie, her bad mood completely forgotten. "Okay."

The three walked to the shop door.

"Where's the stroller?" asked Miss Sissy gruffly.

"Oh, I told Meadow I didn't need it today. Will is a big boy and he does a good job holding hands."

But Miss Sissy apparently didn't trust Beatrice to be the sole protector of Will's personal safety. She quickly grasped the little boy's other hand and looked fiercely down the street in both directions. She snarled at the people in the vehicles and they hastily stopped. Then, head aloft and nose in the air, she carefully walked across the street with Will and Beatrice.

The park was one of Beatrice's favorite places in town and certainly one of Will's, too. Not only did it have nice walking paths and a large toddler playground, but it had an ice cream parlor directly across the street. Sometimes there were bigger kids playing at the playground, too, which provided entertainment for Will—he loved watching them on the rock-climbing wall and the other big-kid equipment.

Will skipped over to the sandbox to play with the front loader truck that lived in the park. Miss Sissy was clearly still in protective mode and barked at another toddler who tried to take Will's truck away from him. The toddler was so surprised at Miss Sissy's raspy voice and rather scary demeanor that he ended up pulling his mother over to play on the swings, instead.

"Sorry about that," called the mom. "I'll talk to him about sharing."

"Bad boy," muttered Miss Sissy, scowling after the child and the mother.

"He's just acting like a two-year-old," said Beatrice with a shrug.

Will must still have trucks very much on his mind after his excitement in the delivery truck earlier. He was happy to stay and play right there in the sandbox with the front loader and a dump truck. When a little girl about his age sat down and looked curiously at the trucks, Miss Sissy made a growling noise deep in her throat.

"She's fine," said Beatrice with a sigh.

And she was. Will handed over one of the trucks and, collaboratively, they rearranged the sand in the sandbox for an hour. They were so absorbed in their task that Miss Sissy even dozed off on a nearby park bench.

Beatrice's phone rang and Meadow was on the other end. "It's taking *forever* here," she said. "They're running very far behind. Is everything okay?"

"Take your time—we're just playing in the park with Miss Sissy."

Now Meadow's voice sounded envious. "That sounds like so much fun. It's such a nice day—far too nice of a day to be stuck in an eye doctor's office."

"It's going to be nice all week, so you'll have plenty of time to enjoy the outdoors."

Meadow hastily said, "They're calling me back now. Finally!" and hung up.

"Looks like you're having a happy day," said a deep voice behind Beatrice.

She turned, smiling, to see Wyatt there. "Well, hi there! I didn't expect to see you out here."

Will, who had somehow managed to get sand in his hair and all over his face, trotted over to hug Wyatt's leg before returning to his sandbox friend. Wyatt didn't seem to even notice that his pant leg was now very sandy indeed.

He sat down on a bench next to Beatrice, which was across from Miss Sissy's. "I was driving by on my way back from an errand and saw you here. Have you heard from Piper at all? I was wondering how she's doing."

"Still achy and feverish, but better. Meadow was watching Will, but had a doctor appointment she needed to run to."

The little girl playing with Will had to leave so Will was at loose ends. Beatrice said, "How about if we go down the slides? Then maybe have some ice cream?"

Will's face lit up and he gave a sandy grin. Beatrice did her best, using items from her large purse, to try to remove as much sand as possible from his face before he trotted over to the slides.

Miss Sissy was somehow still sleeping through it all.

Beatrice said to Wyatt, "I'm never a fan of the big slide when I'm here by myself with Will. It's so much better if someone can help with the stairs and then I can stand at the bottom of the slide. Otherwise, he just goes down the toddler one. He's been dying to try out the big slide.

Wyatt held Will's hand as he navigated up the steep stairs at the back of the slide and then Beatrice caught Will at the bottom of the slide, giving "wheeee!" sound effects to accompany his ride down.

Although running from the bottom of the slide up the stairs and down again didn't seem to wear out Will a single bit, Beatrice was rather tired after a dozen slides. She said, "How about that ice cream, Will?"

Will, as expected, immediately agreed that ice cream would be perfect. Wyatt headed over to wake up Miss Sissy, but the mention of food had permeated through her dreams and she was already headed over to join them.

Beatrice knew chocolate was Will's favorite ice cream flavor so that was an easy order to make at the parlor. But it was harder for her to decide. How did you pick between butter pecan, pistachio, or birthday cake?

She was still mulling over her choices when she noticed Wyatt had already ordered himself a cup of vanilla. Beatrice laughed. "Vanilla?"

He grinned at her. "It's a classic."

"Only when you have two flavors to choose from."

"Sometimes it's nice to keep things simple," he said.

Miss Sissy's strategy was completely different. First off, she wanted samples of five or six different flavors, carefully pondering her choices. Then she went with a triple-scoop combination of three completely different flavors. Beatrice made a face. She couldn't imagine the different ice creams meshing well together.

Finally deciding on a mint chocolate chip, Beatrice settled at a table outside with Miss Sissy and Will. It was hard to tell who was the more enthusiastic eater. Or the messier one. Wyatt and Beatrice appeared positively dainty in comparison.

Beatrice was swabbing some chocolate out of Will's hair when a voice called out, "Well, looka here!"

It was Ramsay, looking tired but happy to see them. Will reached out to give his grandfather a big hug and Ramsay hugged him back. Like Wyatt with the sandbox sand, Ramsay didn't seem at all concerned to be smeared with chocolate. Miss Sissy leaned slightly away from the ice cream-less Ramsay when he sat down, as if suspecting he might reach over and swipe some of hers. "I somehow thought Meadow had Will today," he said in a distracted tone.

"Eye doctor appointment," said Beatrice.

"Ah. That makes sense."

"Any updates on the case?" asked Wyatt.

Ramsay sighed. "It's a real mess, I'm afraid. Unfortunately, we don't have any good leads yet. Did you have a chance to speak with the family about the service arrangements? I'm going to make it to the funeral, of course."

Beatrice knew Ramsay liked attending the services to watch those in attendance and see if there might be any surprises or insights from those gathered there.

Wyatt nodded. "The service will be in a couple of days. It's completely planned out."

Ramsay snorted. "I'm guessing it was Archibald who did that. He seems like the kind of guy who would be a big planner. Do you know Archibald well, Wyatt? I know he's at the church a lot, right? He seems sort of self-contained. I've never really been able to get beyond small talk with him."

"Self-contained is a good word for him. I've spent a lot of time with him on church committees and sat through plenty of meetings with him. But I wouldn't say I really know Archibald. He keeps his private life under wraps. I know he's a very focused and organized guy. He spends a lot of his free time volunteering."

"And it seems like he has *lots* of free time," said Ramsay.

"What is it he does for a living?" asked Beatrice.

Ramsay shrugged. "Some sort of banking work? Remotely, I think? At any rate, I don't think he's done badly for himself. He's hardly amassed the wealth his father had, but he's certainly not in the poorhouse, either."

Beatrice said, "What do you make of Jack?"

Ramsay smiled. "He's an interesting guy."

"He said you and he were in a writing group together," said Beatrice.

"We are, indeed." Ramsay looked at Beatrice. "You seem surprised. Is it because you thought my writing group was full of senior adults?"

"Your writing group *is* full of senior adults. I'm guessing that Jack still fits in really well, though. He seems like the kind of person who can fit into any situation well," said Beatrice.

"You're right about that. Jack is sort of the darling of the group, as you can imagine. He has a remarkable memory—knows each member by their name, asks after their writing project by name . . . it's amazing."

Beatrice thought Ramsay sounded just a bit envious.

"What kinds of things does Jack write?" asked Wyatt curiously.

"Gracious, all kinds of things. He seems like an extremely creative person. If he were just a bit more ambitious, he could be writing slogans and commercials for big corporate customers with a Madison Avenue firm."

Beatrice said in a thoughtful voice, "I'm not sure if I could picture Jack in a corporate environment, even if he *were* ambitious."

"True. I think he'd be bored to tears. He's one of those people who likes being on the move. Working in a delivery truck suits him to a T. He sees lots of different people and goes to lots of different places. I can't see him in a cubicle wearing a suit. He used to be a bit of a handful when he was a teenager, as I recall. Meadow wasn't too keen on having our Ash hang out with him. But he's definitely a talented guy."

Beatrice said, "The whole family seems pretty talented. Mellie is starting up an online quilting business, herself."

Ramsay paused for a couple of seconds. "That's true. And Mellie and Jack seem happy, at least for the most part. I'm not so sure about Archibald and Tilda. They're both fairly somber people and it's hard to tell. You know, there's something about Lester's death and that grimly foreboding house that sounds a lot like a Dickens novel to me somehow."

"There aren't any starving orphans in the house," said Beatrice wryly.

"No, but there are children who've been cut off. And lots of secrets. I think I might want to read *Bleak House* again," mulled Ramsay. "I haven't read that book for a while. That house of theirs sort of reminds me of Dickens. Gothic and gloomy. What are you reading now, Beatrice?"

"Nothing as depressing as that. I wanted a comfort read, so I chose *The Secret Garden*."

Ramsay chuckled. "I guess you don't call cholera and sudden orphaning depressing. Wyatt, I know you've been on a streak of reading work-related stuff. Theological classics?"

Wyatt didn't seem to take offense at the fact that he'd been pigeonholed. Or perhaps he didn't take offense because it was true. "*Why God Became Man*," he said.

"A little light reading." Beatrice smiled at him.

Ramsay tilted his head to the side. "I'm not sure I know that one. Who wrote it?"

"Anslem of Canterbury. It was written about 1098. It's a reread for me."

"Got it. Well, when the author doesn't have a last name, it's clearly an old book." Ramsay chuckled again and then glanced over at Miss Sissy who was glaring at him. The effect was somehow diminished by the fact she had a blob of strawberry ice cream on her chin.

Ramsay cleared his throat. "Miss Sissy, are you reading anything right now?"

"No time!" she hissed at him.

"Right. Busy days, Miss Sissy. Well, good to see you. I guess I should be heading off about now and grabbing something to eat, myself. Let me just give my favorite grandson another hug."

Will happily complied, transferring more chocolate to Ramsay's uniform. Blithely unaware, Ramsay gave them a cheery wave and strode off down the street.

Wyatt gave Beatrice a regretful look. "I should be leaving, too. I need to run by the retirement home and do a little visiting. Do you need anything while I'm out? Need any errands run?"

Beatrice appreciated the offer. As wonderful as Will was and as delighted as he made her, it was certainly a lot more difficult for her to run any sort of errand with him. "I don't think we need anything right now, but thanks."

Wyatt took his leave and then it was just three of them. Beatrice's ice cream was a memory now, but Will and Miss Sissy seemed to savor, and were wearing, every bite.

Beatrice's phone rang again and she picked up. "Meadow?"

Miss Sissy glared at the phone, not wanting her time with Will to be up.

Meadow said in a breathless voice, "Yes, it's me. I felt like I was never going to get out of that doctor's office, Beatrice! Every time the nurse came out to the waiting room, I was *sure* it was my turn. But she kept calling other people."

"Did the other patients arrive after you?"

"Well, no," admitted Meadow. "But it was still most annoying. I suppose the entire office must have been running behind."

The way Meadow spoke, one would think it was a large ophthalmologist office with a tremendous staff of doctors. Instead, it was a tiny place with one doctor. Ordinarily, Meadow was good at entertaining herself while she waited, but Beatrice had the feeling that her eagerness to see Will was to blame for her current impatience.

"Anyway, all's well that ends well. I've got new glasses on order so I can see much better. I don't think I realized how bad my vision actually was! And now I'd like to spend the rest of the day with Will. Are you still at the park?"

"We're right outside the ice cream parlor. I bet by the time you're here, Will is going to be just finishing up with his cup of ice cream."

Meadow said fondly, "He does love his chocolate. I'll be right there."

And she was. Beatrice felt as though she'd just hung up when Meadow was pulling up right in front of them on the street. She hopped out of her minivan and bounded over.

"Will!"

"Granny!" responded Will with perfect enunciation.

Meadow gave him a kiss on the cheek, resulting in a chocolate smear on her mouth. Will was certainly leaving a chocolate trail that was heading all over town.

Miss Sissy made a growling noise.

"Hi there, Miss Sissy," said Meadow cheerfully. "Goodness, but it's nice to see you."

The old woman glowered at her.

"Will, are you all done with your ice cream?"

Will peered down into the empty cardboard cup and nodded.

"Ready to go to Granny's house? I've got a new game for us to play together. It's 'Memory.'"

Beatrice smiled. She had the feeling that Will might have an unfair advantage over both Meadow and herself with that particular game.

Miss Sissy was most dissatisfied by this turn of events. Meadow paused and then reluctantly asked, "Miss Sissy, would you like to join us?"

The old woman spryly hopped up, ready to jump into the car.

"Maybe we should all get the ice cream off ourselves," said Meadow as diplomatically as she could. She pulled out some wet wipes from her massive handbag and handed a few to Miss Sissy. She took a stab at wiping down Will and was able to get most of the chocolate off, despite Will's squirming.

"What are your plans for the rest of the day?" Meadow asked Beatrice as she walked to the car.

"Oh, I think I might do a little yardwork in the front yard. I've got some beds that need to be weeded and I've been acting like they're going to weed themselves." Beatrice mulled some more. "I probably should do a bit of pruning, too."

"Well, at least you have a gorgeous day to do it. Enjoy!" And with that, Meadow bundled the three of them into her car and drove away with a lively honk of her horn and lots of waves from Will.

Chapter Eight

When Beatrice got back to the house, she put on some yard clothes and headed outside with her gloves and Noo-noo, who was glad to spend some time outdoors. The sunlight filtered through the leaves overhead as Beatrice pulled up weeds. It was definitely not her favorite activity, but she liked to see the end results in a tidy bed.

Noo-noo gave some short barks and Beatrice looked up to see Mellie Dawson driving up.

Mellie smiled and raised a hand, making a detour into Beatrice's yard. "Hi there, Beatrice! I'm glad you happened to be outside. I've been meaning to give you a call."

Beatrice stood up. "I've wanted to call you, too, but I know your phone must be ringing off the hook with everyone checking in."

"That's true." Mellie's smile wavered a little and then she suddenly burst into tears.

Beatrice ushered her into the house. "Please, have a seat. Do you like herbal tea? I have some chamomile that's tasty."

Mellie nodded and plopped onto the sofa. Beatrice brought her a box of tissues and then hurried off to make the tea. A few minutes later, Mellie had regained her composure and gratefully took the tea cup from Beatrice.

"I'm so sorry," she started, but Beatrice waved her hand to stop her.

"Mellie, of course you're upset. What a terrible thing to happen to your father."

Mellie took a trembly breath. "It is. But Beatrice, this is the first time I've even cried about my dad."

"I'm sure it was the shock. And now it's wearing off."

Mellie gave her a doubtful look. "I'm not sure. I think it's more that I've been feeling very guilty about not missing my father very much at all. It makes me feel sad."

Beatrice said slowly, "Well, family dynamics are tricky things." She remembered what Ramsay had said about the dynamics between the Dawsons.

"They are. They're very complicated. Believe me, I'm grateful for the upbringing that my dad provided for me. We were given everything and took wonderful trips around the world. We attended concerts and shows at art galleries. We had every opportunity. But I just couldn't seem to forge a warm relationship between my dad and me."

Beatrice took a sip from her own tea. "Some people just aren't very warm to begin with. You might not have been able to be very close with Lester no matter what you tried to do."

"Thanks, Beatrice. I appreciate that. I just can't help but feel that I should have been able to do something more. The worst thing is that my father was murdered. Someone hated him so much that they decided to end his life before it was time for him to go." She took a deep breath. "The police have been asking me lots of questions. It's been pretty scary."

"They're asking *everyone* lots of questions."

Mellie nodded absently. "I know. But they're really focusing on the family. It's making me a nervous wreck. I didn't sleep a bit last night—I ended up getting up and doing housework. I wish I'd had some kind of alibi, but I was home when it apparently happened. My husband wasn't even there because he was out of town on his yearly fishing trip with his college buddies. No one can vouch for me."

"I'm sure no one really has a solid alibi," said Beatrice in a soothing voice. "After all, it was early in the morning."

"True. I just hope Ramsay realizes I didn't have any reason to do something like that. I'm not going to say that my husband and I don't need cash, because that would be a lie. But we're sure not in the position of needing to murder people to get it."

"Of course you're not," murmured Beatrice.

Mellie was quiet for a few moments. She took a couple of sips of her tea and then rubbed Noo-noo, who'd settled at her feet. "I was just thinking about what you said about family dynamics. You're right about them being complicated. And now, with Dad gone, they're about to shift again, aren't they? I just hope that it means we'll all be closer together as a family. I'd really like that. Dad was a great provider, but the same traits that made him good at business made him pretty bad at parenting. He tried to maintain control over us. And some of us are pretty uncontrollable." She gave an unhappy laugh.

Beatrice thought she should try to take the conversation in a happier direction since the whole point of bringing Mellie inside was to calm her down. And she was looking decidedly more agitated. "On a totally different topic, I heard from Posy that you're starting a new quilting business. How exciting!"

Mellie's face cleared and she smiled at Beatrice. "Thank you! I've been really happy about it. The only problem is that the more I learn, the more I realize I don't know very much. I mean, I don't know very much about *business*—the quilting knowledge is all pretty much there."

Beatrice said, "You're doing something with custom quilting, right?"

"That's right. Someone places an order online for a personalized baby quilt for a friend or a quilt for someone who's getting married. Then I sketch out an idea for them to approve. They pay for it and I make the quilt happen. The learning curve has been a little higher than I thought it would be, but I guess starting a business is never really easy." She paused. "I have the feeling I'm going to need to put everything on hold right now, anyway. My mom wants me to help clear the house."

Beatrice watched as her eyes darkened again. "Clear it?"

Mellie gave a short laugh. "Pretty much. Mom has always hated everything in that house. She thinks it's dreary, but my father would never let her change a thing. It's so dark in there—heavy drapes, dark wood furniture, grim artwork. Mom wants me to pretty much pull it all out of there." She rubbed her eyes. "I can't blame her, really. She's put up with it for so long. But she has two other children who could help her. Instead, it's me who has the project. She's pigeonholed me."

Beatrice considered this. She said slowly, "Mellie, I'd be happy to give you a hand with that. It sounds like you're needing to organize an estate sale. Is that right?"

Mellie's eyes lit up. "Really? Yes, that's exactly what I need to do, besides going through all Dad's old papers and books and things."

"I could help you get that set up. I think I'd have a pretty good idea of the value of different artwork and we could find someone to help with the furniture. I have some extra time, too, and can help you go through all the other things."

Mellie burst into tears again, alarming Beatrice. She saw Beatrice's face through her tears and started laughing. "Sorry, Beatrice. But you don't know how much I appreciate it. I've been feeling so overwhelmed with the new business, Dad's death, and then this. You giving me a hand will be such a huge help."

"I'm happy to help you out. I just have to make sure it's not during a time where I need to watch my grandson. Piper has been sick with the flu, but she's on the road to recovery now."

"That's good." Mellie wiped her tears away with a tissue. "I've heard it's bad this year. See, that's the way a family *should* work—supporting each other. I'm just so frustrated with Jack and Archibald." She hesitated for a few moments and then said quietly, "I feel so awful saying this, Beatrice, but I can't help but feel like Archibald might have had something to do with all this. I was planning on calling Wyatt because I've had such bad dreams that I feel I need to talk to someone."

"I'm happy to be an ear for you, if you like, although I'm no Wyatt. He has all the counseling background."

Mellie said, "I think I really just need an ear. I've kept all this bottled up in my head and that's got to be why it's spilling out into my dreams. The fact of the matter is that Archibald had been arguing with Dad a lot lately."

"Have you mentioned that to Ramsay?"

Mellie nodded. "I did, but I thought I was throwing Archibald under the bus. I don't really *like* Archibald and that makes me wonder if I'm just acting out of spite. That's why I wanted to speak with Wyatt—I feel really guilty."

"Is Archibald the kind of person who's argumentative on a regular basis?"

Mellie gave her a smile. "That's exactly why I'm feeling guilty. Because he *is* that kind of person. You could say 'isn't it a pretty day?' and Archibald would say 'there's a storm coming.' That's just the kind of person he is. It could be that the argument I overheard wasn't even important at all or didn't even really mean that much to Archibald."

"Do you have any idea what they might have been arguing about?"

Mellie shrugged. "It was always control of some sort. Archibald always wants to be in charge of everything and so did my father. There was a constant power struggle between them." She paused and said, "You're so sweet to help me out with my mom's house. Thanks so much for that. And here I've been preventing you from working on your *own* house. I'd better head out so that you can get some yard work done."

Beatrice said wryly, "Oh, I'm happy for the break, believe me."

They walked outside and were chatting about lighter subjects when there was a toot of a bike horn and the two women turned to see Georgia, Savannah's sister, getting off of her bicycle. Neither she nor her sister drove a car. With the hilliness of Dappled Hills, it was no wonder to Beatrice how Georgia was in such great shape.

Georgia walked over. "Mellie, I'm glad to see you because I've been meaning to call. I was so sorry to hear about your dad."

Mellie gave her a tight smile. It was clear that she really didn't know how to react to the sympathy she was getting. "Thanks, Georgia. I appreciate it."

Georgia immediately picked up that it was a tough subject and moved on to another. "Hey, Posy told me about your quilting business. Congratulations!"

"Thanks," said Mellie a little shyly. "I thought it might be a good way to earn a little extra income. I'd been working for a while waiting tables, but my feet weren't really up to it. It's funny—I can walk with no problem, but as soon as I stand still a lot, they really bother me. So I had to find something to do that didn't involve standing up all day."

Georgia said, "Oh gosh, I can imagine! I'm on my feet a lot teaching school, but I've gotten used to it. When I first started, my feet were killing me." She paused and asked, "Do you have a website set up for your business? Or are you using one of the established retail sites like Etsy?"

Mellie flushed a bit, the stress that had been written on her features earlier making a return. "That's one of the things I'm trying to figure out. I know I've got to do something, but I've been going back and forth about how to handle it."

"You could have an online retail shop *and* host your own website. It wouldn't hurt and might be a nice way to show up in the search engines. SEO—Search Engine Optimization—and that kind of thing."

Mellie looked even more lost at the mention of SEO. Her eyes widened, just thinking about it.

Georgia said, "I'd be happy to help you out with setting it all up, if you like. I make bow ties and outfits for pets and have had an online shop for a while—my husband, Tony, helped me set it all up and now I manage it all on my own. I'd be happy to give you a hand at your house, if you like."

Mellie looked a little alarmed at the idea of Georgia coming by. Beatrice wondered if Mellie had been so busy with everything lately that her house might be messier than she liked. "How about if we meet at the Patchwork Cottage? It's so cheerful there and Posy has a good internet connection and a table for us to work on."

"Sounds perfect. I'll give you a call and we'll figure out a time." Georgia gave them a cheery wave and cycled away.

"Thanks for everything," Mellie said warmly to Beatrice. "Do you think you can possibly help me out tomorrow with my mom's house?"

"That should be absolutely fine. I'll just check in with Piper and Meadow to make sure babysitting is covered."

"Just let me know if anything changes. My schedule is totally flexible right now. Talk to you soon!" And with that Mellie hurried off to her car.

Beatrice continued her yardwork, taking a little more time doing it since she had so much on her mind. As she was finally finishing up around her mailbox, she heard a car approaching and straightened to see Wyatt pulling into the driveway.

He stepped out of the car. "Hey there," he said, coming over to give Beatrice a hug. "The yard looks fantastic. I feel bad that I wasn't here to help you, though."

"Oh, it's such a beautiful day that I wanted to spend some more time outside. Being with Will in the park today just whet my appetite for more sunshine, I guess. And it's good to get a bit more exercise while I mull things over."

She and Wyatt walked in, arm in arm.

"What kinds of things are you mulling over? Did you hear some more about the investigation?"

Beatrice said, "Well, Mellie stopped by the house. She mentioned that she might want to speak with you, by the way."

"Should I reach out to her?"

Beatrice said, "I'd probably just wait and see if she gives you a call. She spent a good deal of time talking to me today and maybe that will hold her for a while. I think she might just have wanted to get some things off her chest." She paused. "I'm actually going to help her tomorrow with clearing out Tilda's house."

Wyatt raised his eyebrows. "Really? How much clearing is Tilda thinking about?"

"I have the feeling, from what Mellie was telling me, that it might be a massive job. Tilda is apparently envisioning making the house a lot more cheerful by replacing the dark furniture, removing old artwork, and lightening things up."

Wyatt frowned. "That sounds like far too much for just you and Mellie. Isn't Tilda pitching in?"

"I got the impression that Tilda wanted to assign it to Mellie and have it be her responsibility. That's why I thought I'd lend her a hand. At the very least, maybe I can help her get everything ready for an estate sale and help her decide what to do with the things in Lester's old office."

Beatrice sat down and Wyatt sat next to her. "That's really kind of you, especially considering being in her father's office where Lester was found might be very upsetting to her."

Beatrice nodded. "Mellie seems to have a lot going on right now with the new business and now her father's death. I'll try to lighten the load a little bit."

They sat together, thinking about Mellie. Noo-noo, seeming to sense the sober mood, trotted over and nudged Beatrice with her nose. Beatrice called her and Noo-noo leaped up to drape herself over both their legs, lightening *their* load a little bit.

Chapter Nine

The next morning, Beatrice was cleaning up the breakfast dishes when she got two phone calls in rapid succession. The first was from Meadow who'd let her know that she was going to have Will for the day (and that Piper was still a bit weak, but better). The next was from Mellie, checking in to see if Beatrice might be available that morning.

After getting ready, Beatrice headed out for Tilda Dawson's house. As she approached the house on the long driveway, she felt as if there was almost a menacing presence surrounding the property. She was irritated with herself for being fanciful. It was a house like any other house. A place to live and that was it.

Still, the entire place had a gloomy feel to it, from the sightless windows covered with heavy drapery to the cold stone of the exterior.

Beatrice felt a little cheered when Mellie answered the door, opening the solid structure wide to let her in. "Thanks *so much* for coming," she whispered to her, giving her a tight hug. "I don't know how to thank you."

"I'm happy to do it," said Beatrice in a similar whisper, wondering if Tilda was within earshot. It seemed unlikely because she certainly wasn't within view and it was such a tremendous house. "How is everything here today?"

"My mother has a headache," said Mellie with a sigh. "She's lying down." Then she raised the volume of her voice a bit after a short laugh. "Sorry. I don't know why I'm whispering. Somehow the house feels so oppressive to me. Maybe that's why. I almost feel like I'm in the library or in church or something—that I need to stay hushed."

Beatrice followed Mellie into the foyer. They looked around them from that point, surveying the antique furniture in every nook and cranny, the portraits and grim landscapes on the walls and all the way up the staircase in rows, and the heavy drapes and oriental rugs.

Mellie rubbed her forehead. "Beatrice, I don't know what I was thinking. This is far too big a job for us. What do people do when they're facing something like this? I don't even know where to begin?"

Beatrice was sure that's why Tilda outsourced the job to Mellie. Tilda wanted it all gone, but didn't want to be the one to make it happen. "Well, there's definitely going to need to be an estate sale, of course. I think the wise thing to do would be for me to quickly move through the house with you and assess if there's anything you'd like to keep from the house. Or anything your mother wants to keep, of course."

"Mom has already been very clear that there's *nothing* she wants. But there might be one or two pieces that I wouldn't mind taking home." Mellie's face, however, was doubtful as if she couldn't immediately picture what those might be.

"Good." Beatrice pulled a legal pad and pen out of the tote bag she'd brought with her. "Let's go through every room. Tell me what you might want to pull aside. And I'll give an assessment about any artwork that I think is particularly valuable and might generate more income from an auction than an estate sale."

"I'm so glad you're here," breathed Mellie. "I was freezing up just trying to figure out where to start."

"I don't think that first part will take long. Then we can get started with the easier things—clearing out personal effects of your father's. I'm guessing those might be the first things your mom would want to go, since they can be the hardest things to part with."

Mellie's face was again doubtful, but she eagerly nodded. "Whatever we need to do to keep on track."

"Then we should get in touch with someone who can organize the sale and tag the items. We'll need a professional appraiser."

"From Dappled Hills?" asked Mellie worriedly.

"There will be some regional ones. I'll check into it for you."

Mellie smiled at her. "Thank you. I don't know what I'd do if you weren't here to help. Probably badger Archibald into figuring out what to do."

For the couple of hours, Beatrice and Mellie walked around the house. Mellie noted the items she was interested in and Beatrice took a closer look at the artwork and made notes in a notebook.

When they'd finished that, Mellie said, "I guess we'll move into Dad's study."

Beatrice noticed that her entire demeanor changed. "I know this has got to be so tough on you. Are you sure you're ready to tackle it today?"

"I think I want to just get it over with without thinking too much about what I'm doing." Mellie hurried off to find garbage bags. Considering the number of bags she came back with, Beatrice wondered if Lester's office was a huge disaster.

When Mellie opened the door, however, it wasn't. Lester had a massive mahogany desk with absolutely no personal effects on it—no photos of his children or his wife. No knick-knacks. No pens or pencils, even. It was so stark-looking that Beatrice wasn't entirely sure where to start.

Mellie directed her, this time. "Do you mind starting with his desk? Sorry. I'm thinking it might be better for me if I can start with boxing up his books. It's a little less personal."

It definitely was. Beatrice wished she were the one dealing with the books. "Of course I will," she said instead.

But she immediately hit a roadblock when she found a couple of the drawers were locked. "Do you know where the key to the desk is?"

Mellie had to stop and consider this. "Let's see. I wouldn't think he'd keep them very far away from him." She looked around the room carefully. "He would have wanted it to be convenient for him to open."

Beatrice looked around, too. She noticed the books were all perfectly lined up on the shelves . . . except for one, which seemed to be jutting out a little.

Mellie followed the direction of her gaze and walked over to that section of the built-in bookcase. After pulling the book out, she saw it was hollow. "Good eyes, Beatrice."

She handed the keys to Beatrice. Before Beatrice could use them, they heard a voice calling from downstairs. "Anyone here? Hello?"

Mellie frowned. "Who is that?" She abruptly stood and hurried off for the stairs with Beatrice following her.

When they walked down the stairs, they saw that Imelda had intercepted the visitor. And Imelda seemed decidedly displeased with the small, dark-haired visitor with the grim mouth.

Imelda quickly said, "She walked in on her own! And she won't leave. I said it wasn't a good time."

"It's okay, Imelda," said Mellie firmly. "Thanks for trying to help. I've got it from here." Imelda stalked away and Mellie continued, "Is there something I can help you with?"

The woman nodded. "I'm Laura Ellis."

At first, Beatrice wasn't sure if Mellie realized that Laura was her father's daughter. But then she nodded. "Of course. How can I help you?"

A cold voice came from upstairs. Beatrice turned to see Tilda standing there, roused from her nap but without a hair out of place. "You can't help her at all, Mellie. If Laura needs help, she should speak with our lawyer and not with us. And you should leave at once. I don't know how you got the impression that it would be all right for you to trespass."

Laura said coolly, "I would have knocked, but I had the feeling I wouldn't have been allowed in."

"This is intolerable," said Tilda in an icy voice. She stalked off to leave Mellie and Beatrice to handle the unwanted guest.

Mellie gave Beatrice an uncertain look as if needing cues on how to proceed. Beatrice said quietly, "Up to you, Mellie."

Mellie straightened her shoulders and said pleasantly, "Won't you come sit down?" She looked over at Beatrice. "Please stay for this?" Beatrice nodded.

Laura followed Mellie into the great room with Beatrice hanging back a little. Laura looked around her as they walked, taking in everything.

They sat down in the formal room, all looking as stiff as they clearly felt. Mellie gave Beatrice a pleading look.

Beatrice cleared her throat. "Is there something you're needing?"

Laura said wryly, "I suppose a relationship with my sister is too much to ask."

Mellie made a choking noise and Beatrice looked over at her with worry. Suddenly overwhelmed from either the day's activities, Laura's unannounced visit, or both, she gave Beatrice an apologetic look and rushed out of the room.

Laura knit her brows and looked down at her hands, folded in her lap.

Beatrice sat and patiently waited for Laura to say something.

"I suppose it's a bad time," said Laura finally, as if there would be a *good* time for her to pay a visit.

"I expect so," said Beatrice.

Laura looked up and said curiously, "Are you a member of the family?"

"No. I'm Beatrice Thompson. I'm a friend of Mellie's. My husband will be the minister officiating at the service."

Laura looked a bit more at ease following this explanation. "You're the preacher's wife. Got it. And you know the family."

"To a degree," said Beatrice cautiously, not sure where Laura was going with this.

"Could you hear me out for a few minutes? I really could use someone to just listen to me and see if what I'm doing is appropriate."

"I don't know if I'm the best person to comment on that," said Beatrice uneasily.

Laura gave a short laugh. "Believe me, you're the best option I've got. I don't exactly have a lot of friends in this town." She decided to launch right into her monologue to override any objections Beatrice might continue to broach.

"Lester Dawson was my father. I must have the poorest timing in the world, but I'd come up here to speak with Lester, convince him to acknowledge me, and persuade him to give me some sort of help. I definitely wasn't expecting him or any of the family to warmly welcome me and invite me to be part of the family, but I also wasn't expecting to arrive and find that Lester had been murdered."

Beatrice said, "Of course you weren't. That must have been very difficult for you."

Laura gave a small shrug. "It would have been worse if I'd actually known him. I was under no illusions that it would be a happy homecoming, as I mentioned, but I didn't realize I'd end up in the middle of a murder investigation. I'd driven over to the house yesterday morning to try and speak with my father. I saw all the police vehicles—and they saw me. I suppose the police drew their own conclusions."

"You believe they're considering you a suspect?"

"Absolutely. They've likely dreamed up some motive that I'm the disaffected daughter who was rejected by her father and killed him for revenge." Laura shrugged again but Beatrice could tell by her expression that the idea of being a suspect was scary to her.

"How long were you in town before Lester's death? Were you able to make contact with him earlier?"

Laura shook her head, looking frustrated. "I've been here a week or so, but he hung up on me when I called, slammed a car door or a house door in my face, or otherwise indicated he had no intention of speaking with me."

Beatrice sat quietly again, letting Laura have a few moments.

Laura continued, "It hasn't been the easiest year. My mother died a few months ago after a long battle with cancer. That's why I chose now to finally go see my father. I knew it would upset Mom if I went to see Lester and the last thing I wanted to do was to hurt her, especially in the final stage of her life."

"I'm sorry about your mom," said Beatrice softly.

Laura's eyes filled with tears and she looked down at her hands again. After regaining her composure, she said tersely, "Thanks. Like I said, it's been a hard year. But I wanted to reach out to Lester. I felt like he owed me some recompense. Or, if not me, my mother, for all the trouble and expense of raising me on her own. Now I'm all alone in the world. And, yes, I was contacting my father to make sure he offered me some sort of support. But I also wanted to make a connection with him—and

with my half brothers and sisters. But you saw how that went."
Laura blinked rapidly.

Beatrice carefully said, "You might want to reach out again
later. It's just not an easy time right now."

"Of course it isn't. But I'm only in town for so long." Laura
paused and then said, "I just can't believe the police think I
could have murdered Lester. Why would I have wanted to hurt
him when I was hoping to get some financial support from him?
And a relationship, too. It's all just such a mess."

Beatrice said, "It sounds as if Lester knew who you were
right away. Did you introduce yourself to him when you arrived
in town?"

"I actually sent him a letter first. Believe it or not, I'm usually not the sort of person who just shows up out of the blue. I
reached out to him, explaining who I was, sending a picture of
myself, and asking if we could meet."

"And did you hear back from him?" asked Beatrice.

Laura nodded, giving a tight smile. "He sent the letter back
in pieces with a terse note telling me to stay away."

Beatrice sighed. "That must have been awful."

Laura swallowed and Beatrice could see exactly how much
his rejection had hurt. "It was pretty bad. I don't know why I expected more—my mother had briefed me on the type of man he
was. She never wanted me to try and contact him. I guess I was
just optimistic, or maybe just hopeful. That's when I thought it
might be better if I reached out in person . . . it would be harder to get rid of me, I reasoned. Besides, the way he'd handled my
letter made me really angry. I just dropped everything and headed here to confront Lester."

Beatrice said, "Did he tell his family about you? Sorry, it just seemed as if they might know who you were, even though you clearly hadn't been invited in the house."

"He must have. They all seem to know who I am, even if I don't know who they are." Laura's face was dejected.

Beatrice thought how strange it would be to have a family of siblings and not even know who they were.

Laura continued, seeming to read Beatrice's mind, "I did look online to see what I could find out about my brothers and sister. Archibald had the biggest online footprint."

Beatrice gave a wry smile. She was sure that was probably true. She could see Archibald making sure his online profile for work and the church and other organizations was completely impeccable. He was so meticulous that he likely was even careful about people tagging him in photos, ensuring that everything online was exactly the way he wanted it to be.

"Archibald actually approached me on the street when I was downtown yesterday," said Laura.

"Did he?" Beatrice had the feeling that it wasn't a social visit.

"He was very brusque. He told me my being here wouldn't change anything and it would be best if I left town. That my presence here was upsetting his mother." Laura swallowed.

Beatrice thought about the calm and collected Tilda. If she was upset about anything, it certainly wasn't showing. But then, Jack had said she did a good job hiding her feelings, so it could be that Laura's appearance in town was more disturbing than she let on.

"At least Archibald *has* a mother," said Laura bitterly. "Mine is gone and my father, too. Now I have no one."

Laura grew quiet and she and Beatrice sat for a few moments in silence. Then Laura continued, "Mellie is the one I'd like to establish a relationship with. She seems like such a warm person. There wasn't much about her online at first, but then I saw all this quilting-related stuff. I'd love to learn how to quilt." Her voice was wistful and her gaze trailed off to the staircase where Mellie had disappeared. Drawing her attention back to Beatrice she added, "I couldn't find out much on Jack, either. He was on social media, but he had it locked down so only friends saw his posts. I didn't think it was a good idea for me to ask to be his friend."

Beatrice said, "Again, I think I would give this some time. The family may only recently have found out about you. Plus, they're trying to process Lester's death."

Laura nodded briskly. "I'm sure you're right. I've always been an impatient person, I guess, and this is just one more example. I always want to make things happen quicker than they do in their own time." She paused. "What do you make of Tilda, by the way? Aside from just now, I haven't had the chance to even lay eyes on her."

Beatrice demurred. "I'm not sure it's my place to say, Laura. Plus, I don't know her very well."

Laura raised an eyebrow. "Spoken very diplomatically—just like a minister's wife. I have the feeling that Tilda is also coming under scrutiny by the police. Isn't it usually a spouse who's responsible when someone has a mysterious death? After all, Lester was apparently serially unfaithful to her. I know my mother said that she and Lester stopped seeing each other because he had someone *else* on the side. And then there's that woman that Lester was seeing—Shirley. I saw them both in town together, so I know he hadn't stopped his extra-marital activities. When I saw Tilda a few minutes ago, even from a distance, it felt like there was all this repressed fury in her."

Beatrice thought it likely that at least some of the repressed fury might have had to do with Laura's unexpected and imprudent appearance at the house, but didn't express this opinion.

Laura continued in a thoughtful voice, "It seemed like she was icy, but I felt that she had all that built-up anger in her that was truly powerful. She had a lot to lose if I'd convinced Lester to change his will, of course."

It hadn't sounded to Beatrice as if Lester was in any danger of changing his will in favor of Laura. From what Laura had said, he'd avoided her at every opportunity.

Laura rubbed her face. "This is all such a mess. I hate to think Tilda has something to do with all this, but she does really have some motive. Thinking back on Shirley, the woman who was involved with Lester. I know she's also looking for accommodations in Lester's will. Maybe she was pressing Lester to rewrite his will and include her in it. Tilda might have been tempted to make sure the old will was the last one."

There was the noise of a door opening upstairs and Laura abruptly stood. "I guess I'll come back another time."

Beatrice nodded and walked her to the door. As soon as the heavy front door shut behind Laura, Mellie came cautiously to the top of the stairs. "She's gone?"

Chapter Ten

Beatrice nodded and Mellie's shoulders relaxed as she came down the stairs to join Beatrice. "My mother has taken to her bed. I'm so sorry you had to deal with that by yourself, Beatrice. Was it awful?"

"Not really. I got the impression that Laura just didn't think about the timing of her visit. She was mostly frustrated that she hadn't been able to meet with your father when he was alive and that her efforts to reach out to him had been rebuffed."

Mellie said wryly, "No surprise there. My father wasn't the biggest fan of being taken by surprise. Or in developing relationships. It was hard enough spending time with him as one of his children he *did* acknowledge." She paused and flushed a little bit. "I think the whole family has been thinking that Laura is here to wrangle some money out of us. Not that she isn't entitled to something. Did she mention money at all?"

Beatrice said, "I think she feels like she's owed something. Of course, she'd planned on trying to reason with your father. Things became more complicated when Lester passed away."

Mellie sighed. "It doesn't make sense that Laura would have murdered my father, does it? She would have been more likely to get some sort of money from him if he were still living. The family thinks that she's the one responsible for Dad's death. Her or Shirley."

Beatrice wasn't surprised to hear that the family was fixated on it being someone outside their group.

Mellie shrugged. "I mean, unless Laura flew into some kind of rage with my father when he wouldn't provide for her? It's hard for me to picture that, though. Laura seems like a really calm and collected person, not the kind who suddenly flips out and kills someone in a rampage. Right?"

Beatrice nodded. "The primary emotion I've noticed from her seems to be frustration. She's impatient that things haven't gone according to plan. And part of her plan was to develop a relationship with you."

Mellie's face flushed. "With *me*?"

Beatrice nodded again. "It sounds like she's all alone in the world right now. Her mother died not long ago from cancer and that's what motivated her to try and meet your father. She said she never would have wanted to do it when her mother was alive because her mom was very much against it. So it didn't sound like she was just here for financial reasons. I'm sure she wanted to try and forge a relationship with Archibald and Jack, too, but she especially mentioned you and having a sister."

Mellie blinked at this and looked thoughtful. Beatrice wondered if maybe she was equally interested in having a sister. After all, she had two brothers—having a sister would make for a completely different experience. Beatrice continued, "I explained that the family had a lot to process right now and it probably wasn't something that was going to be able to happen right away."

"Well, that's certainly true. Every time I start to get used to one reality, something else happens. It's finally starting to sink in that my father is gone. What with the police talking to us all the time and trying to get the house in order, everything is hard to digest. Anyway, thank you, Beatrice, for everything. I'm sure I wouldn't have been able to handle Laura as nicely as you did and I really don't want to offend her. I hope she understood when my mom and I ran off today."

Mellie shifted uncomfortably on her feet and then added, "I have the feeling we should call it a day. I'm sorry to ask this of you, but do you think you can come out another time to help me tackle Dad's office? I don't think I'm up to it today, and I know my mother probably isn't up to any more chaos. Her headache is making her pretty miserable."

"Of course I can come back another time. Don't think a thing of it—I'm happy to come back and help. You've had enough to deal with today. Besides, I think we've made real inroads already."

Mellie smiled at her. "With your help."

As Beatrice left the house, her phone started ringing. She climbed into the car and answered it.

"Edgenora?" she asked.

The church secretary answered, "Hi, Beatrice. I'm so sorry to bother you. Are you in the middle of something? I was wondering if you had any time to run by the church for a little while and lend a hand."

"Originally, my day was going to be taken up by something, but my schedule just unexpectedly opened up. What's going on?"

Edgenora said, "Unfortunately, a couple of our clothing closet volunteers have been hit by the flu and aren't able to make it over. There's a good-sized pile of donations to sort and I thought it might be better for them not to come back to such an overwhelming task when they should be taking it easy."

"Good point. Sorry about the flu—it's definitely making the rounds."

"How is Piper doing?" asked Edgenora.

"Much better, thankfully. But she hasn't had a fun time. Okay, I'll be right over there."

A few minutes later, Beatrice pulled into the church parking lot and walked into the church office. Beatrice thought it was a comfortable and comforting space with its booklined walls, scattered throw rugs over the dark wood floor, and softly padded chairs.

Edgenora gave her a relieved look when she walked in. "Thank heavens you're here. Old Mr. Taylor is driving in from Lenoir in a couple of hours and he would have made the trip over here for nothing if those clothes aren't sorted. I tried to reach him on the phone, but he's very tough to get in touch with. I'm not totally sure he knows how to even operate his cell phone."

"No problem at all. It's just lucky that my day opened up when it did."

"What were you *supposed* to be doing?" asked Edgenora. "Might you have to step away again?"

"Oh, no. No, I was helping Mellie out at Tilda's house. We reached a stopping point." Beatrice reflected that it was more of a crashing halt.

Edgenora nodded. "That reminds me that I've been meaning to send a card or some food over to Tilda."

"I think Tilda's in good shape with food, but I'm sure she'd appreciate a card or a note."

"It must have been awful, Lester's death coming out of the blue like that. Especially the fact that he had such a violent death. She must be very shaken up," said Edgenora.

Beatrice wouldn't have put it exactly that way, but then everyone grieved differently. "The whole situation has been hard," she said diplomatically.

Edgenora added in a hushed voice, "Well, I'm sure it doesn't help that a particular neighbor of mine has been making a nuisance of herself. I'm sure she's driving the Dawsons crazy. Has anyone from the family mentioned Shirley?"

Beatrice nodded. "That's added to a stressful situation, for sure. I didn't realize Shirley was your neighbor."

"Do you know her?" asked Edgenora carefully.

"No, I've just spoken to her briefly."

Edgenora sighed. "Well, between you and me, I was sort of appalled by the situation. Apparently, Lester Dawson paid the mortgage for the house. At least, that's what Shirley told me."

"She told you about their arrangement?" This surprised Beatrice a little bit. Even though Shirley had told Beatrice about it, Edgenora often looked so stern that she couldn't imagine Shirley sharing such personal information with her.

Edgenora nodded and said crisply, "She certainly did. She didn't seem at all concerned by the fact that she was a home-wrecker. And now she says she's fallen into arrears on the mortgage."

Beatrice frowned. "How on earth did that happen? Lester just passed away and he didn't seem like the kind of person to be late paying the mortgage."

"Apparently, they had some sort of tiff a couple of months ago and Lester decided not to pay it."

Beatrice asked, "Wouldn't that hurt Lester more than Shirley? In terms of his credit, I mean."

"The mortgage is apparently in Shirley's name—Lester just paid the bank. Until he didn't."

Beatrice raised her eyebrows. "That must have been quite a tiff."

"Oh, they used to argue all the time. I was amazed that she yelled at him just as much as he yelled at her."

This was indeed a surprise, especially considering the fact Shirley talked about how well she and Lester got along together.

"Sounds as if they were quite a couple. I hope Shirley's situation resolves," said Beatrice.

"So do I," said Edgenora glumly. "Of course I don't want her to lose her home, but I also wouldn't want the house directly next door to me to go into foreclosure."

"Fingers crossed it won't. Well, I'd better get to that sorting," said Beatrice, glancing at her watch.

She walked into the storage room where the clothing donations were kept and worked as quickly as she could to sort men's clothes from women's and children's. Shoes went into another container. Some of the items had been rather optimistically donated and were in poor enough condition to go into the trash. She was relieved to have another woman join her after a little while. The two had just finished up by the time Mr. Taylor walked in to take the load to Lenoir.

Beatrice chatted with the old man for a few minutes, helping him load the clothing into his truck. Then she set off for home.

When she got into the house, she realized she was exhausted. All-in-all, there had been a lot of work going on that day. She curled up with Noo-noo on the sofa. "We'll just take a short nap," she said to the little dog.

Noo-noo seemed to agree with her and soon they had both fallen asleep. When she woke up again, she felt rejuvenated. This was a relief because sometimes when she napped, she felt a bit worse when she woke up than before she'd fallen asleep. As if she'd been awakened in the middle of the night or something. But feeling very alert this time, she immediately started getting some household tasks out of the way before checking on Piper.

Piper sounded much more like herself, to Beatrice's relief.

"I'm feeling a hundred percent, Mama. Finally. It took a while though. What's going on with you? I feel like I've missed out on everyone else's lives. Almost like I'm Rip van Winkle or something."

Beatrice laughed. "More like Sleeping Beauty, I think."

Piper said wryly, "If you could see me, you wouldn't say that. I'm at the point where I'm ready to get cleaned up and put my makeup on. But seriously, how have things been?"

"Well, it's been something of a mixed bag," said Beatrice. She filled her in on Lester Dawson's death.

Piper said, "I'm so sorry to hear that. Well, mostly sorry for Mellie, who's really the only person I know in the family. But Archibald is very involved in the church, I think, so you probably know him, too."

"Wyatt knows him better than I do." Beatrice had the feeling, from what she'd heard from others, that she actually wasn't particularly interested in getting to know Archibald any better than she did. She turned back to the subject of Piper's health. "Now, I'm going to give you some motherly wisdom, whether you're ready for it or not."

Piper laughed. "Lay the wisdom on me."

"Take things *slowly* as you're getting back into your usual activities. Regardless of how well you feel, recovery from the flu can take a while. Don't jump right back in or you might find yourself right back in the bed again."

Piper said in a rueful voice, "You know me well. Looking around the house right now, I see all kinds of things that need to be done. Ash did his best, of course, but he's just not in a regular routine of keeping the house organized."

"Just let things stay messy for a while," urged Beatrice. "And let Meadow spoil you with the food she's bringing over. You know she enjoys it."

"And I'm finally enjoying it, too, now that my appetite has come back. Thanks, Mama."

The rest of the day was a peaceful one. Wyatt came back from the church and they had a nice supper together with ingredients Beatrice had pulled together randomly in a pasta. They listened to music and read their books quietly in the living room that evening until they turned in.

The next morning started just as peacefully. Wyatt and Beatrice drank some coffee while reading the paper and working on puzzles. Wyatt was on his way out the door to head to the church when Meadow appeared on the doorstep.

"Good morning, Meadow," he said cheerfully.

"Is it?" asked Meadow distractedly. She reached down to rub Noo-noo who had trotted over to greet her.

"Is something wrong?" asked Beatrice.

"Ramsay just told me that Shirley Keller is dead."

Chapter Eleven

"What?" chorused Beatrice and Wyatt.

Meadow nodded. "Yes. And it was murder. That's all Ramsay could or would tell me about it. I probably wouldn't even have found out that much if I hadn't been there when he got the call. Isn't it awful? That poor young woman."

Wyatt nodded grimly. "It is awful. I'm sure Ramsay will get to the bottom of it soon, though. I'm sorry, but I've got to leave you two and walk over to the church."

"Of course," said Meadow in that same vague voice, stepping aside to allow Wyatt to get past her.

Beatrice said, "Come on in and have a seat, Meadow. Can I get you some coffee?"

"All the coffee," said Meadow with a sigh as she plopped down on the sofa. "I just can't believe this is happening again."

Beatrice brought in some mugs of coffee, sugar, and cream on a tray and put it on the coffee table. She said, "Wyatt was right, though. Ramsay will soon figure out what's going on. Unfortunately, it does sound as if someone in the family is responsible, doesn't it?"

"Well, I'm *sure* it's not Mellie," said Meadow rather heatedly. "It must be someone else in that family."

Beatrice hid a smile at Meadow's rabid protectiveness of anyone in the quilting community.

Meadow continued, "Maybe it's Archibald. He's always so grim. Plus, he seems like a planner. Wouldn't you have to be something of a planner to successfully carry out two murders and not immediately be apprehended?"

"I'm not sure." Beatrice took a thoughtful sip of her coffee. "From what I've picked up, it sounds like it could possibly have been a spur of the moment thing. That maybe someone acted out of rage. Plus, no one really knows what goes on inside a family, even if they seem like very decent, ordinary members of the community. The Dawsons, in some ways, are pretty unusual."

"I don't think the family is *unusual*, exactly. I think what's happening around the family is what's weird. The whole Shirley thing was fairly scandalous for a town like Dappled Hills. But I'm very sorry she's not around anymore. I suppose she must have known who killed Lester, don't you think? Unless *she* killed Lester and someone from the family murdered *her* to avenge Lester's death."

Beatrice said, "I'm not sure it's the kind of family where someone would have necessarily wanted to avenge Lester's death."

"No, you're probably right. Lester wasn't hugely popular inside the family, was he?" Meadow sighed again. "It's just all so discouraging. At least Piper is feeling better."

"Yes, I talked to her yesterday. I told her to make sure she didn't try to do too much or she might end up relapsing."

Meadow eagerly nodded. "Exactly! That's what I was telling her, too. Because she's just itching to get up and put the house back in order again. I tell you, Ash certainly didn't do a wonderful job with the housework. He was trying to do everything and wasn't doing any of it particularly well. He's a smart man! What is it about laundry that's so inexplicable?"

"He had trouble with the laundry?"

Meadow waved her hand around, endangering both the coffee she was holding and Beatrice's sofa. "Oh, he got the washing and the drying parts right. But he didn't separate by color because he was in a hurry and the whites ended up dingy-looking. Then he didn't put anything away, which everyone knows is *part* of the entire laundry process. There are three parts—wash, dry, put away." Meadow sat back on the sofa, looking aggravated.

"His heart is in the right place, Meadow. He's probably just overwhelmed with everything he's had to take on while Piper was sick."

"Yes, but now is not the time to slack off when Piper still needs to be resting. I think I'll head over there and clean up this morning while Ash is out of the house because he might not appreciate my following up behind him. Ash is about to take Will to preschool, so it should be the perfect time."

Beatrice had the feeling that although Piper would definitely appreciate the house being clean, she may not particularly want her mother-in-law to be the one to get it in that condition. So she quickly said, "Actually, that's my plan for the morning, besides heading over to the church. Why don't you cook again for Piper, instead? She was saying on the phone how much she enjoyed your cooking, especially now that she's feeling better."

Meadow preened at the compliment. "That's very sweet of her to say. Oh, I know—I'll make her some shrimp and veggie pasta. She loves shrimp, and some protein would do her good right now. I should go ahead to the store while it's still early."

And with that, Meadow disappeared just as quickly as she'd arrived.

Beatrice gave Piper a quick call. "Hey there. Just wanted to give you a heads-up that I'm coming over to do a bit of cleaning up this morning."

"Oh, Mama, you don't have to do that."

"Yes, I really do. Because if it's not me, it's going to be Meadow."

Piper gave a chuckle. "I see. Okay then—thank you."

Beatrice said briskly, "The only rule is that you're not allowed to help whatsoever. You need to just stay in bed and rest."

"But I feel so much better. Resting is going to be difficult to do," said Piper ruefully.

"I know it is, but that's your project for the day—resting. I'll be right there."

And Beatrice was. But because the mess was only a few days' worth, the cleaning was fairly matter-of-fact and went quickly. There were clean clothes to fold and hang (Beatrice put them back in the dryer for a few minutes to get the wrinkles out first), the dishwasher to empty and fill again (and run again), and junk mail to dispose of.

She stuck her head in to check on Piper, but she was peacefully sleeping, an open book on her chest. Beatrice slipped out of the house, locking the door behind her.

Then she set out for the church for the yoga class she kept trying to make and somehow kept missing. She even had her yoga mat in the car, which was progress since that was another thing she kept forgetting.

As she got out of the car in the parking lot, Beatrice spotted Archibald and Wyatt standing together at the entrance to the church.

"Hi there," she said as she approached them.

"Yoga today?" asked Wyatt, taking in Beatrice's yoga pants and long top.

"That's right. I thought I should at least try and make one out of every three classes," said Beatrice ruefully.

Archibald said in his matter-of-fact manner, "Wyatt and I were just finishing up the arrangements for my father's funeral."

"Is there a date set?"

Archibald nodded. "We're having it day-after-tomorrow at noon. Then a reception will follow, of course."

"Oh, at the church?" asked Beatrice.

"No, Mother wants to host it."

Beatrice wondered if this really was the case or whether Archibald had pushed the issue. As far as she could tell, Tilda's focus appeared to be on clearing the house and redecorating it.

Archibald said grimly, "On a different matter, I suppose you've heard about that woman's death."

"Shirley Keller?" asked Beatrice. She realized she shouldn't be startled anymore by the entire family's directness, but it was hard to get accustomed to.

"That's right. Of course, it's a terrible thing." Archibald's cold tone wasn't particularly convincing.

Wyatt nodded soberly. "It's always incredibly tragic when young people die. And Shirley's death is especially so because it wasn't a natural death."

"Her death does, however, save us from having Shirley at my father's service, which would have been an awful slap in the face to my mother. But then, on the downside, the police appear to be questioning the family again. Wanting to know where we all were." He gave a derisive snort. "Like all respectable people, we were asleep at that time, of course."

Beatrice said, "Did the police offer you any details, then?"

"Only from the aspect of trying to find out where *we* were. But yes. It was late at night. She was apparently pushed down a steep staircase in her home."

Wyatt said, "It was definitely a push, then? It couldn't have been an accident? Maybe Shirley stumbled when she was on her way downstairs to get a drink of water or something."

"Oh no, the police were very firm on that point. There was some sort of blunt force trauma involved. Anyway, she met her end very late at night and, being good citizens, the family had all quietly turned in."

Beatrice said, "So no one had an alibi."

"No. And since my wife and I are currently separated, I don't even have a basic one. I suppose Mellie's husband will at least say they were together." Archibald had a brooding look about him.

Wyatt said gently, "I'm sorry to hear about your separation."

"Yes. Thank you. I'm sorry, too. I have every hope that we might be able to make it back together, though. After all, every marriage goes through tough spots and that's all this is."

There was a slight questioning note in Archibald's tone that Wyatt quickly picked up on. "Yes, marriages often do have rough patches."

Archibald gave a brief nod of acknowledgement. He looked brooding again. "It never would have happened if my father hadn't gotten involved."

Wyatt and I glanced at each other. Beatrice said, "Involved how?"

"In something that wasn't his business. He knew I'd had an . . . indiscretion." He continued briskly, "It meant nothing and it was over practically before it began. However, it was wrong. I've asked both God and my wife to forgive me."

"And your father knew about it?"

Archibald gave another bob of his head. "He did. You see, my father believed it was absolutely vital to get leverage on people. He would sometimes employ private investigators to dig up dirt on all of us." He said this in a matter-of-fact manner as if that were something that happened in every family. Wyatt and Beatrice glanced at each other again.

Wyatt said, "The private investigator followed you around and found out about your . . . indiscretion?"

"That's right. And my father couldn't wait to let me know about what he'd discovered," said Archibald, sounding bitter. "It didn't matter to him that what the investigator had seen was me breaking up with the woman I'd been briefly seeing. My father didn't care about me trying to piece my marriage back together. He just wanted to wreck it. I don't think he'd ever really liked Blaire." His mouth twisted unhappily.

"Lester called her up to tell her?" asked Beatrice. She couldn't wrap her head around the disfunction in the Dawson family.

Archibald acknowledged this with a curt nod. "Blaire was devastated, of course. But angry, too, and justifiably so. I never wanted to hurt her—she wasn't supposed to know about my illicit relationship at all. It was just my father's attempt to insert himself into my life in an unpleasant way."

Wyatt said, "I'm sorry to hear how it all unfolded with Blaire. Please feel free to call me anytime if you and your wife would be interested in any counseling of any kind."

"Thank you." Archibald gave a short laugh. "Considering everything going on, I might even come by for *individual* counseling. This thing with Laura is out of control, too."

"Is it?" asked Beatrice. She'd ended up feeling rather sorry for Laura by the end of their conversation together. Considering she'd just lost her mother, the only parent she'd ever known, it must have been incredibly hurtful to be rejected by her father and then immediately lose the opportunity to establish any kind of a relationship with him.

Archibald turned to look at Beatrice. "I understand that Laura came by while you were at the house helping my mother and Mellie. I'm sorry you had to deal with that. I hear you were left on your own with her." His lips pressed together in displeasure.

"It was perfectly fine. Your mother and Mellie were upset by her arrival and I was happy to speak with Laura."

Archibald tilted his head to one side, looking at her through narrowed eyes. "Did she tell you what she wanted? Why she was there? It seems like an odd thing to do—interrupt a grieving family by showing up at the house uninvited."

Beatrice carefully said, "I got the impression that one of the main things she was there to do was to try and establish a relationship with the family."

Archibald stiffened. "Well, that's not going to happen. I have no interest whatsoever in expanding the family to include her. Can you imagine having Thanksgiving and Christmas with your father's illegitimate child in attendance? What would that do to my mother? It doesn't bear thinking about." He paused. "And money? I suppose she must be wanting some sort of money. Perhaps she's fallen on hard times." He shrugged and looked mildly discomfited. "Perhaps she's always *experienced* hard times."

Beatrice said, "I think that's something you should speak with Laura about."

Archibald had that brooding look again. "I suppose the Christian thing to do would be to settle some sort of sum on her." He looked questioningly at Wyatt.

"That would be up to the family, of course. Perhaps if Laura needs some financial support and there are no provisions made in your father's will, the family could discuss it."

Archibald didn't look particularly pleased by the prospect. "I have the feeling Jack and Mellie might not be fully onboard with the idea. They're not exactly financially stable themselves, either one of them."

Beatrice offered, "Mellie was filling me in on her new business venture. It did sound promising."

Archibald snorted. "Did it? It sounded a little 'pie in the sky' to me. Mellie doesn't know anything about business whatsoever."

"She does know about quilting, though, and that's half the battle." Beatrice realized her voice was a little cooler than she'd intended it to be.

Archibald looked from her to Wyatt and then sighed. "You're absolutely right. The important thing is that Mellie is trying, at least. As her older brother, I really need to be more supportive. Speaking with my minister and his wife is a helpful reminder to be more charitable when speaking of others."

Archibald paused and then added reluctantly, "Maybe I need to be more generous when speaking of Shirley, too. You're right, Wyatt, it was tragic for her to lose her life at such a young age. I will say that she seemed to make my father happy, at least some of the time they were together. And when my father was happy, the rest of the family was happy—especially my mother. She hated having a stormy atmosphere in the house and was always so relieved when everything was peaceful."

Beatrice said, "The police definitely thought her death was tied into your father's?"

Archibald nodded grimly. "I asked that straight away and they confirmed it. The only reason that I can think of for Shirley to have been targeted is if she knew something. After all, she was either on the property or nearing it when my father died. Perhaps she saw Laura, still trying to make contact with us." He brightened a little. "We wouldn't have to settle any money on Laura if she's involved. She can't profit from a crime."

Beatrice was suddenly tired of speaking with Archibald and just as suddenly aware that she'd missed some of her yoga class. "I'm sorry, I'm going to have to run to my class. Wyatt, would you like to grab lunch together after I'm through?"

"Sure—I should be in my office then."

Beatrice hurried off, leaving the two men to continue their talk at the front of the church.

Beatrice never liked going to yoga, but she really enjoyed having *gone* to yoga. She felt so much more relaxed and focused once the class was over. She'd thought to bring a change of clothes with her in her tote bag, so she changed into something a little more lunch appropriate and headed over to Wyatt's office.

Chapter Twelve

Wyatt smiled at her and stood up to give her a hug as she came in. "You look nice."

Beatrice chuckled. "You sound surprised."

"I somehow thought you'd still have your exercise clothes on. Did you run home to change?"

"No, I brought clothes with me, hoping you'd go to lunch with me. Where should we go?"

Wyatt considered this. "Well, we've mostly been doing picnics and meals at the church lately. Why don't we go to that new restaurant that opened recently? The one with the French name? *Chez* something."

Beatrice quirked an eyebrow. "Sounds fancy."

"Yes. And likely fairly expensive, but it shouldn't be for lunch."

They decided to try it. The restaurant owner had gone all-out with the decorating. There were reproductions of old masters' paintings on the walls, a beautiful tile floor, and heavy wooden tables and chairs.

"Mercy," said Beatrice.

Wyatt looked slightly nervous himself. "They didn't post the menu on the window."

"I wonder if it's the kind of menu that doesn't list prices on it."

Wyatt grimaced.

They were quickly seated at a table covered in a spotless white tablecloth and handed a menu. Fortunately, there *were* prices on it and luckily the prices *weren't* too steep for lunch. But there was another problem.

"It's in French," said Wyatt in a slightly appalled tone.

"No worries," said Beatrice airily.

"You speak French?"

"My phone does," said Beatrice.

And it did. Which was how they were able to order a couple of delicious items off the menu with very little trouble.

Wyatt took a happy sip of his Provençal fish soup. "This hits the spot. And it's healthy, too. We'll have to come back here another time"

Beatrice nodded as she finished off her crepe. "Delicious. This crepe is so thin, but really flavorful at the same time. It's amazing."

They felt so positive about their healthy meals that they decided to split a dessert. The dessert, however, was in the decadent category, which decidedly messed up what they'd achieved with the healthy lunch. The crème brulee had a delicious melted sugar crust with a creamy custard inside. There was a hint of lemon zest.

While Wyatt was paying the bill, a tremendous storm blew in with sheets of rain, sudden crashing thunder and lightning, and clouds so dark it made it look like the end of the day.

Wyatt grinned at Beatrice. "It's a good thing you parked directly in front of the restaurant."

There were other customers gathered at the door, waiting for a break in the rain in order to make a run for it. But the rain showed no indication of letting up long enough for anyone to dash to the car without getting completely soaked.

Wyatt pulled up the local radar on his phone, studying it for a few moments. "I think we'll just have to brave it. It looks like Dappled Hills is going to be socked in for the next hour or more."

"We'll be fine," said Beatrice briskly. "After all, we're only a few steps away from the door."

However, a few steps were all it took in the unrelenting rain for them both to be completely soaked.

"I'll drive you home to get changed," said Beatrice.

They looked at each other and laughed. Their hair was flattened to their heads and they were sitting in puddles of water that had collected from their clothes.

"It looks like we've been swimming," said Wyatt.

"Fully dressed," agreed Beatrice.

They drove home in the pounding rain and hurried inside the house. Noo-noo, who was never a fan of storms, fireworks, or anything sudden and loud, was hiding under the coffee table, trembling. She cautiously stuck her head out and gave them a mournful look.

"Sorry, girl," said Wyatt. "I've got to head back to work. Your mama is going to give you some love as soon as she gets dried off."

Wyatt changed quickly, grabbed an umbrella, and then hurried out to his own, dry, car to drive the short distance to the church.

Beatrice came back into the living room to join Noo-noo who was still shaking. Her brown eyes looked up at Beatrice in concern.

"Here, love. You'll be all right. Let's find your thunder shirt." Beatrice pulled out a tight-fitting garment for the little dog, meant to calm her down and make her feel safe when she was scared. Then she pulled her up on her lap on the sofa and felt Noo-noo's body relax. "It's okay, girl. It's loud, isn't it?"

And it was loud. The thunder and lightning, one right after the other, continued for the next thirty minutes. Beatrice put on some soft music to make their environment a little less-scary. Then, finally, the thunder let up, although the rain continued pelting down. Noo-noo curled into Beatrice's side and, exhausted, fell right to sleep.

After their nap (Beatrice fell asleep shortly after the corgi did), the rest of the day passed blissfully quiet with lots of reading (Mary just discovered the secret garden) and quilting (Beatrice was able to use up even more of her scrap collection). She put together breakfast for supper, which was a favorite of both Wyatt's and Beatrice's. They spent a quiet evening together as the rain moved in again. The quiet night and turning in early was a good thing because the next morning was a quilting workshop at the Patchwork Cottage. It was actually part of the Village Quilters guild meeting, but the community was invited to attend.

After Wyatt left for work the next day, Beatrice got ready to head over to Posy's shop. She wasn't immediately excited about the workshop and hoped she might get more interested when she got over there. Posy was going to be discussing fabric dyeing, and Beatrice wasn't at all sure that she wanted to dye anything. It seemed far too messy a process for Beatrice's liking.

When she arrived at the shop, she saw that quite a few people *did* seem to be interested in fabric dyeing. There were plenty of Village Quilters there, as well as quite a few members of the Cut-Ups guild, too. To her surprise, Mellie Dawson was also in attendance. Beatrice walked over to greet her. "It's good to see you here."

Mellie gave her a wry smile. "I'm trying to get better at certain techniques in case I need them for my new business. Do you do any fabric dyeing?"

"Me? Goodness, no. But I'm interested in seeing the quilts Posy brought in to demonstrate the technique. She always does a fabulous job."

Mellie asked, "Did you bring a quilt?"

Beatrice frowned. "Oh, mercy. We *were* supposed to bring a quilt for the sew-and-tell portion, weren't we? I've had so much going on lately that it totally slipped my mind." She bit her lip a little, abashed. "Not that *you* haven't had a lot going on, Mellie."

Mellie gave her a sad smile. "I think focusing on quilting has been a good technique for me to keep my stress level down."

Posy gently called the meeting to order, effectively stopping the myriad conversations taking place around the room. "Hi everyone. Thanks for coming. A special greeting to our honorary Village Quilters members who've come to hear more about fabric dyeing."

The Village Quilters all politely applauded their guests.

Posy continued, "What we'll do is skimp on the business portion of the meeting so we can get right to our workshop."

She read the minutes of the last meeting, talked about upcoming events, and gave a wrap-up of a service project they'd recently worked. They'd made fidget quilts for Alzheimer's, dementia, and autistic patients. Then they had the sew-and-tell portion for the quilters who'd brought a quilt with them.

When it was Mellie's turn, she stood and held up a quilt that was beautiful, but made Beatrice immediately think of storm clouds. Mellie said in a soft voice, "Some of you have known me for a long time since I grew up here. I was a pretty unhappy teenager, which I guess isn't so uncommon among teenagers."

The quilters gave a gentle laugh.

"Anyway, I wasn't happy at home and I wasn't happy at school, either. I always felt like I didn't quite fit in. Then one of my high school teachers, an art instructor, introduced me to the art of quilting. It made such a tremendous difference in my life. For one thing, it was the perfect hobby to help me de-stress. Plus, I made friends because the teacher got several other students into quilting. We'd spend time together after school in the teacher's room, quilting and talking about designs, fabrics, and ideas for different projects. The creativity and the sense of community was what got me through my teen years. This is one of the quilts I made during that time."

Everyone clapped again and Mellie sat down, beaming.

The workshop went very well. Posy demonstrated some of the techniques and held up some quilts that incorporated fabric dyeing. It wasn't quite as messy as Beatrice had thought it might be, although she still wasn't sure it was something she wanted to try herself. She liked seeing the end results, though.

Once the workshop and meeting were over, Beatrice and Mellie stayed to help Posy clear everything up.

"Mellie, you really don't have to do this. Nor you, Beatrice. I can handle it," said Posy, protesting.

Mellie said, "If I weren't doing this, I'd have to be knocking off things on my to-do list that I'm not quite ready to tackle."

"Same," said Beatrice.

Many hands made light work and soon everything was put back to order. The women took a seat in the sitting area of the shop to catch their breaths. The shop cat, Maisie, jumped up on the sofa next to Mellie and Mellie absently stroked her.

Posy frowned. "Where was Meadow today?"

"She's giving Piper a hand with Will today. Piper is feeling a lot better, but she really needs to rest in order to fully recover."

"I'm glad she's feeling better," said Posy. She turned to Mellie with a smile. "I loved hearing about your quilt. What a caring teacher you had!"

To Beatrice's and Posy's dismay, Mellie burst into tears.

"Oh, dear," said Posy, her kind eyes full of worry.

"I'll find some tissues," said Beatrice, glad to have a mission. When she returned with a box, Posy was sitting with Mellie and the shop cat on the sofa, her arm around Mellie.

Mellie gave them both a rueful smile. "I'm so sorry. I promise I'm not usually an emotional person."

"Don't apologize to us," said Beatrice. "You've had so much to handle lately. Stress can be so overwhelming."

Mellie nodded. "It is. And it's coming from so many different directions. But you're right, Posy—it was so meaningful to have an adult in my life who cared about me and tried to come up with solutions for my unhappiness. She's the best. I wrote her a long email just a couple of years ago thanking her for the lifeline she threw me."

"Such a kind thing to do," murmured Posy.

"*Everyone* has honestly been so kind. Georgia helped me out with setting up a website and also listing my business on one of those craft marketplaces online. I don't think I realized how much work was going to go into setting up the business online. I was totally focused on the quilting part of it."

Beatrice said, "I'm sure there's a lot that you wouldn't know about until you really started setting up the business."

"Then, of course, there's been everything with my father's death. There again, though, everyone has stepped in and been wonderful. I haven't had to cook a meal since my father died. And Beatrice, you were such a tremendous help with the house."

"I'll come back whenever you're ready to start again," said Beatrice. "How is your mother doing?"

Mellie shrugged. "She does seem to be getting a little better. She's completely absorbed in her plans to redecorate the house so she has a collection of magazines she's always looking through. She wants it brighter and airier with lighter colors and softer window treatments. My mother talks about it all the time. It's almost as if she has a fully-developed plan for the house and everything she wants to implement."

Posy said, "Maybe she's been thinking about it for a long time?"

"Absolutely. I think she's been wanting to make changes to the house for decades but knew my father wouldn't hear a word of it. Or maybe she's just thrown everything into planning to forget about all the unpleasant things that are happening right now."

Beatrice asked quietly, "Shirley?"

Mellie nodded.

"How is she handling that news?"

Mellie sighed. "I suppose like we all are. We're impacted because the police have been asking us questions again. I was hoping Meadow would be at the workshop today so I could quiz her on what Ramsay thinks."

Posy said slowly, "I'm not really sure Ramsay *tells* Meadow what he thinks."

"He definitely doesn't seem to fill her in during investigations," added Beatrice.

"That's what I was afraid of. I couldn't sleep last night for worrying about it all. The police have tied the two deaths together and our family really seems like the target of their investigation." Mellie absently rubbed Maisie and she purred and brushed her head against Mellie's hand.

The bell on the door rang and Posy stood to see who was coming in. "Oh hi, Edgenora!"

Edgenora gave them a wave. "I'm just browsing, Posy. Go ahead and sit for a spell. Sorry I couldn't make the workshop today."

"No problem. I know you were working at the church this morning," said Posy.

Posy sat back down and Mellie added, "Anyway, it's just been really stressful and Shirley's death has sort of compounded things."

Beatrice asked, "Did you know Shirley at all?"

"Not a bit," said Mellie immediately. "I'd never even met her and no one in the family did, either. She'd called once, I think, but that was it. Of course I'm sorry that she's dead, but it's not as though I was personally invested in her. I just wish we had decent alibis so the police could focus on somebody else. I mean, who's to say it was a planned murder? Maybe Shirley surprised a burglar or something. Maybe my father did, too."

Posy said sadly, "A good alibi would definitely help."

"I only wish I'd known I needed one. My husband was asleep and I was downstairs working on my website—late." She gave a short laugh. "The police think I slipped out the door, headed over to Shirley's, and quickly got rid of her before heading home and turning in as if nothing had happened."

Posy's brow crinkled. "I don't understand why they think you would have wanted to kill Shirley at all."

Mellie hesitated, realizing Posy didn't know all the details of what had happened. "Well, she seemed to think she had a right to some of my dad's estate because of a relationship she was in with him."

"Oh." Posy colored.

Mellie continued, "I'm really worried about my family. I thought the one good thing that might come out of my father's death was that we would all feel somewhat freer. That we wouldn't have that heavy weight that we'd carried for so long. My father was a very controlling, stern man. I loved him and I'm sorry he's gone, but I really hoped we'd all feel less stress in our lives. But now, we're more stressed out than ever."

Beatrice gave her a sympathetic look. "It's been a lot to deal with."

"Definitely. Mainly because of the police investigation and the way it's making us look at each other with suspicion." She rubbed her eyes tiredly. Then she said, "Oh, Beatrice, I wanted to ask if the church might be interested in my dad's suits. He had closets and closets of them and they're in excellent condition."

"I'm sure the clothes closet would be very grateful. Professional clothes for interviews and other special occasions are really helpful. I'd be happy to run by and pick them up from the house for you."

"Thank you. My mother will be very relieved to get rid of them, I'm sure."

Beatrice added, "Do you think you're ready for me to come back over and give you a hand with the other stuff?"

"I think so, if you're up to it. Maybe we could just get started with one room and then you could take the suits? When do you have free time?"

"I'm free today, if that works for you. I have an errand or two first and then I could run by."

"That would be great, Beatrice. Thanks so much to you again. I think I might be getting into the swing of things with it all. After you give me a hand with one room and the suits, I'm going to do another walk-through after . Sort of like what you had me do before. But this time, it'll just be me trying to assess how much stuff we're talking about. I keep finding closets and chests and things. I need to make an estimate for how much time this might take so I can budget it. I don't want any surprises. I have the feeling the attic is full, too," she said morosely. "I'll be glad when all this is over. Starting a new business while being a suspect in two murder investigations isn't easy."

She looked at her watch and sighed. "Looks like it's time for me to be heading out." She gave Maisie a final, regretful rub and stood up. "Thanks for hearing me out. It makes me feel better to talk about all this."

"Of course!" said Posy.

"Anytime," said Beatrice. "See you in a little while."

After Mellie left, Posy and Beatrice looked at each other.

"It's just so sad," said Posy, sensitive to others' feelings as always. "Poor Mellie is going through such a rough time. I can't imagine losing a parent and then having to deal with a murder investigation."

"And starting a business at the same time. It's pretty brutal."

Posy said, "Why do the police think the family is involved? I don't really know the rest of Mellie's family."

Beatrice said, "Well, I'm sure they think the motive boils down to money. I get the impression that Lester had lots of it and might have been stingy about sharing it with his family. The police might think that he was killed because it would be an easier way for the family to access his money."

Edgenora came around the side of a notions display, looking a bit conflicted. "I hope you two won't think I was eavesdropping."

Posy said quickly, "Oh, you can't help but overhear things in this shop. I listen into conversations all the time without meaning to."

Edgenora sat down on the sofa and absently rubbed Maisie, who purred loudly and gave her a loving look. "It's just that I heard Mellie say something that wasn't exactly true. Perhaps she forgot the details or something. Stress can do that to a person, I know."

"Mellie misstated something?" asked Beatrice.

"Yes, a misstatement. That sounds better. It's just that Mellie said she hadn't met Shirley Keller. But she had."

Chapter Thirteen

Beatrice and Posy looked at each other.

"Oh, dear," said Posy.

Beatrice said, "I'm guessing you'd seen Shirley and Mellie in a conversation?"

Edgenora nodded. "I'm afraid so. I was Shirley's neighbor, as you know, so I observed all sorts of things going on over there." She blushed. "Again, it sort of makes me sound as if I'm a snoop."

"Not at all," said Beatrice. "I can't help but notice what goes on with my neighbors, too. It's only natural. You get used to observing people's routines and their comings and goings. It's what helps keep a neighborhood safe, actually."

Edgenora looked relieved. "Yes, I suppose it is. Anyway, I find it a little hard to believe that Mellie had forgotten about meeting Shirley. They were engaged in quite an argument right before Shirley's death."

"Oh, dear," offered Posy again.

"Do you have any idea what the argument was about?" asked Beatrice.

Edgenora shook her head. "It was quite animated, though. It was on Shirley's doorstep—she didn't invite Mellie in—and Mellie was crying when she left. I thought about going out to make sure she was okay, but then thought that might appear a little intrusive. I felt terrible for Mellie, though, because she looked so upset."

"And Shirley?"

Edgenora sighed. "She looked upset, herself. I've had a little less sympathy for her, but I certainly hate what's happened to her. She was a young woman who was in over her head with that family. She took on more than she could handle."

They sat quietly for a few moments. Then Posy said slowly, "I just can't imagine that Mellie would have anything to do with Shirley's death. Wouldn't that also mean she was involved in her own father's death, too?"

"Not necessarily," said Edgenora in her brisk manner. "It could simply mean that she had other motives to eliminate Shirley. Money, for one. I know Shirley needed it. But Mellie probably needs it, too."

Beatrice said, "It is definitely expensive to set up a new business. And hasn't Mellie's husband had sort of a scattered work history?"

"I think his work history has a few gaps in it," said Posy sadly. "I know Mellie has mentioned being stressed about it in the past. He's some sort of a manager and I guess managers are sometimes the first to be laid off. Although that's certainly not *his* fault. Anyway, I'm sure Mellie couldn't have had anything to do with *anyone's* murder. I just hope the police will see things the same way."

Beatrice asked Edgenora, "Did you tell Ramsay about this?"

Edgenora rubbed at her temple with her free hand, still stroking Maisie with the other. "I haven't yet. I was hoping Mellie might say something to Ramsay, herself. It sure would sound better coming from her. And maybe there's a completely reasonable explanation."

"I'm sure there is," said Posy quickly.

Beatrice could only hope so.

They visited for a few more minutes before Edgenora mentioned the type of fabric she was in the shop looking for and Posy got up to help her find it. Beatrice headed out to get some birdseed at the local hardware store nearby. The feeders that Posy and her husband Cork had made for her had gotten rather low on seed.

The hardware store was one of those very old-fashioned shops which fit Dappled Hills to a T. It sold glass bottles of RC Cola, various seeds, local honey, and gardening supplies. It was the kind of place where you could get your kitchen knives sharpened, your tools repaired, or your keys copied. The old hardwood floors were a bit warped with age and creaked as you walked. The staff was always friendly and helpful and knew where everything was.

Beatrice walked up to one of the workers, an older man with a long beard and twinkling eyes. "I'm here to pick up birdseed. But the reason I'm needing so much birdseed is because the squirrels have been wiping me out. Any ideas?"

"Oh the squirrels are holy terrors, aren't they? If you put some safflower seed in the feeder they're picking on, I think you'll see some improvement. They're not crazy about eating saf-flower."

Beatrice thanked him and headed over to the seed section to peruse the offerings. The bell on the door rang and Tilda Dawson came in. As always, she was dressed impeccably in tailored blouse and slacks. Her face was drawn, making the lines there look deeper. She spotted Beatrice and came right over to speak with her.

Tilda came straight to the point, as the no-nonsense person she was. "Thank you for intervening in our family drama yesterday. I'm so sorry you were put in that position. I wasn't feeling very well and just wasn't up to dealing with that young woman. And I've heard that Mellie wasn't any help, either."

"I was happy to help out," said Beatrice. "I'm not even sure I was even all that helpful. I just listened to Laura for a bit and then showed her out afterward."

Tilda flinched a little at the mention of Laura's name. Her mouth curled up slightly. "Well, that's more than Mellie or I were able to do." She hesitated. "What did the young woman have to say?"

"Well, she was interested in forming a relationship with you ... with the family, I mean. I got the impression she has no one who's really close to. Her mother is gone now."

There was a little twitch again around Tilda's eyes at the mention of Laura's mother. "I see."

An uncomfortable silence occurred. At least, it was uncomfortable for Beatrice, although Tilda seemed rather unmoved. Beatrice finally grabbed hold of a topic. "How are things at the house going? I'm actually running by there right after this to bring Lester's suits to the church's clothes closet and give Mellie a hand with some of the other clearing out."

"Gracious, I should thank you for that, too. Mellie told me you'd also helped with the value of some of the artwork and other pieces. I've already mentally moved on to the next stage where I'm considering paint colors, fabric swatches, and things like that. I've found it makes an excellent distraction from everything else going on. I was actually looking for someone to do some painting for me, once I settle on a shade. Do you know of anyone?"

Beatrice nodded. "We've used a gentleman named Dan at the church and he does great work. I could text you his number."

"Would you? I appreciate that. I have the feeling I need to get on his calendar before it fills up."

Beatrice scrolled through her contacts, found Dan's information, and then texted it over. She knew it was going to take some time before the house would be ready for paint, but she understood Tilda's impatience for making the house her own.

A voice called out, "Look who's here!"

Beatrice didn't even have time to look up before Meadow bounded over, rather like Tigger in the Winnie-the-Pooh stories.

"I saw your car outside, Beatrice, and realized I've been needing for ages to pop by here to buy lightbulbs. How nice to see you both!" Meadow reached over and gave Tilda a big hug, which Tilda stiffly endured. "How are you holding up?"

Tilda said, "I'm all right. Thank you, Meadow."

"Are you? Because things in Dappled Hills have simply not been right lately. I haven't been able to sleep at night with all this nonsense going on."

Beatrice found this very unlikely. One of Meadow's gifts was her ability to squeeze out a good night's sleep in any situation. It was something Beatrice was very envious of.

Meadow continued. "And I'm sure you're in a similar situation, Tilda. I'm just so *sorry* about everything you've had to deal with lately. Good for you for getting out of the house and maintaining a stiff upper lip. I heard about Shirley—so awful. Really ghastly to have another death in town." Then Meadow had the grace to blush, realizing Tilda may possibly not want to discuss her husband's other woman.

Tilda said in a somewhat robotic voice, "I really don't know anything about that. I didn't know Shirley, of course. Why would I?"

Meadow, still quite red in the face, said, "Of course you wouldn't. So awful."

Tilda continued, "I was at home, as I told your Ramsay, sleeping. Or trying to, at any rate. As you mentioned, sleep can be hard to come by when you have a lot of stress. The doctor prescribed something to help me drop off since things have been so hectic lately. I'm not crazy about the medicine, though. It makes me feel sort of sluggish and hungover in the morning."

"Maybe he can adjust the dosage or find something else that works better," suggested Beatrice. "Change always makes it difficult to sleep and you've certainly endured so much of it lately."

Tilda gave a bob of her head. "I'm hoping staying busy in the daytime will help, too." She looked over at Meadow. "Like I said,

I never even encountered Shirley. Never met her. What's more, none of my family did, either. Please do reinforce that message to Ramsay for me."

"Of course I will," said Meadow quickly.

Beatrice knew that Tilda either didn't know about Mellie's argument with Shirley or was covering up for her daughter. Edgenora stated that not only had Mellie met Shirley, she'd clearly not had a peaceful encounter with her.

Tilda continued, "Anyway, back to staying busy. The probate process has been keeping me busy, for sure. Archibald has been helping me to organize papers for the courthouse. It's clearly going to be a very long time before some of these funds are freed up."

Beatrice nodded. "Probate can take forever. I remember when my first husband died, it was really tough trying to juggle probate while raising Piper and trying to work at the same time. Fortunately, most things were in my husband's *and* my name."

Tilda sighed. "That's the way it *should* be. Unfortunately, Lester had a very old-fashioned view of roles in a marriage. Everything was in his name, so there's going to be quite an estate account. Archibald is planning on helping me to make the process go as quickly as it can, since some of my children have a cash-flow problem."

Meadow said cheerfully, "Well, that can be the way when our kids are just starting out."

Beatrice thought that was a charitable thing to say since Tilda's kids weren't exactly in their early 20s.

Tilda gave Meadow an absentminded smile. "Maybe I'll need to lend them some money for a little while."

Meadow clearly approved of this plan. "Good for you! Sometimes our kids need a little help. Just because they're adults, it doesn't mean that they don't need our help from time to time. And isn't it nice to be needed again? It makes me feel absolutely wonderful. Beatrice and I have been helping Piper and Ash because Piper is recovering from an awful bout of the flu."

Tilda took a couple of subtle steps back as Beatrice hid a smile.

"Well, I'm sure things will work out in the end. It's just terribly stressful going through all this right now. I have faith that Ramsay will get to the bottom of it all," said Tilda.

Meadow said enthusiastically, "Our Beatrice is a wonderful investigator, too. Ramsay thinks she's marvelous. Amateurs can really help a lot."

Tilda looked at Beatrice with interest. "Good for you. I mean that. I really need to consider what I'll do in the next phase of my life. Although I don't think investigating murders will be on the list."

Meadow said, "Well, that's what you're here in the hardware store, isn't it? You're trying to move forward and make a few changes. You're doing a great job."

"Getting the house updated is nice, of course. But I'm thinking more of new chapters in my life. Decorating the house is only going to take so long, you know."

Beatrice said, "It seems like you're really enjoying the process, though. You're basically coming up with an entirely new way of picturing your home."

Tilda nodded. "Visualizing it has been fun. And, of course, I've been keeping my ideas in a notebook so I can keep track of them all."

Beatrice said, "Have you thought about the possibility of doing decorating as a hobby? Or even as a part-time job? I know money really isn't an issue, but it might be rewarding to be paid for something you're good at and are interested in."

A spark lit in Tilda's eyes. "I hadn't thought of that. What an interesting idea. And it would certainly get me out of the house a bit."

Meadow said, "Oh! And Mellie could even set up a website for you, now that she's figured out how to do it for her own business."

Tilda nodded. "You're right. Thank you, ladies. You've really given me some food for thought. And now I should let you run your errands while I get my decorating odds and ends."

Meadow picked up her lightbulbs and Beatrice her birdseed and then they headed out of the hardware store while Tilda was still discussing paints with one of the employees.

Out on the sidewalk, Meadow said, "I'm awfully glad to see Tilda's icy façade melt just a little bit. I swear she didn't used to be that way. She was a lot warmer and more accessible."

"Maybe she needed to put up some protective barriers after Lester passed. After all, she has a lot to deal with. It could be her way of processing it all."

Meadow nodded. "You're probably right. What are you doing now?"

"I'm going to be heading over to give Mellie a hand with her father's clothes for the church clothes closet."

"That's going to be a big job, I bet. Do you need me to help out? Lester was always dressed very fine whenever I saw him," said Meadow. "I think he was the kind of person who put on a suit every day, even if he was just going downtown to get a haircut."

"I think Mellie and I will be able to handle it, but thanks. His wardrobe should make for a huge boon for the clothing closet. They love getting interview clothing or special occasion clothing. But yes, I got the impression it's going to be a lot of work. On the upside, I should sleep well tonight."

Beatrice took her leave, throwing her birdseed in the backseat and heading over to the Dawson house.

Chapter Fourteen

Mellie let her inside. "Saw you drive up through the upstairs window. Beatrice, you really are a gem to give me a hand like this. It would just be so completely overwhelming otherwise."

"Oh, I'm totally happy to help. I remember what it was like when I moved to Dappled Hills from Atlanta. I thought my house was so organized and that I really didn't have that much extra stuff. Then I started packing, and I couldn't believe what I'd collected over the years. I had old college letters and notebooks neatly boxed up and labeled. But I'd never looked at them again—it just was tough to get rid of them."

Mellie said ruefully, "I have the feeling we're not going to be in quite the same boat since we don't really have quite the sentimental attachment to my dad's things. How did you work through your memorabilia, though?"

"I went through every bit of it, which took forever. I ended up taking pictures of things I wanted to 'keep' and then tossed all of the paper. Now I can look at it when I want to, but I don't have the stacks of letters and notebooks. And it keeps Piper from having to worry with all my papers after I'm gone."

"Great idea," said Mellie as she led the way upstairs. "And even though I don't have the emotional connection to my dad's things, there are items that will probably remind me of him. Maybe I should take a picture of those."

"Only if they'll make you happy. I wouldn't take a picture of anything that would make you feel sad or conflicted in any way."

They walked into Lester's office and Beatrice felt a chill go up her spine even though she'd already been in the room during her last visit to assess the artwork. Lester had passed away in the room but it was almost as if his presence was still there among the heavy wooden desk, the dark leather chair, and the collection of rather grim-looking books.

Mellie seemed to feel the heaviness in the room, too. She sighed as if there was a lot of pressure on her. "You know, I used to play in this room when I was little. Always when Dad was out of town or still asleep, of course. He wouldn't have been crazy about anyone being in here—it was supposed to be off-limits to everybody. I remember his desk had all sorts of nooks and crannies in it. I think it had a secret compartment, too."

Beatrice said, "It sounds like you do have some good memories here."

Mellie sighed again. "Sort of. I think I was also looking over my shoulder the whole time worried I was going to get caught." She took a deep breath and squared her shoulders. "Okay. Let's get started."

"What area would you like me to work on?"

Mellie considered this. "How about if I start with Dad's desk and you tackle his file cabinet over there?"

Beatrice hadn't even noticed the discreet file cabinet that melded into the background. She nodded and got to work.

About fifteen minutes later, Mellie said, "I'm going to have to play music on my phone or something. The atmosphere just seems so heavy in here. I know it's my imagination working overtime, but it's distracting me."

Beatrice said, "Of course—whatever makes this easier for you, Mellie."

Mellie scrolled through her phone and soon there was cheerful pop music from the 80s playing. The upbeat sound did seem to make the work a little more palatable even though it was out of place in the somber room. Beatrice was literally knee-deep in old contracts from decades earlier. Mellie still looked sort of pale, so Beatrice tried to engage her in some small-talk. "How are things going with the new business?"

Mellie's shoulders relaxed a little. "Oh, it's going okay. I actually got my first order earlier today."

"Really? That's great, Mellie!"

She laughed a little. "Don't be too impressed. It was somebody local that Posy knew. But it's a good way for me to get my feet wet, you know? It'll be easier for me to consult with them about what they're looking for. Plus, they probably won't be too demanding, unlike complete strangers online."

"I'm glad to hear that there are at least some things that are going well for you."

Mellie said, "Thanks. It's been a tough time and not just in the last week. You probably didn't know this, but my husband got laid off from his job."

"I'm so sorry, Mellie. That must have created a lot of stress for you. Is he employed again now?"

She shook her head. "Not yet. At first it seemed like he was going to be okay, but as the weeks have gone on, he's been more and more despondent. It's like they say—men's identities can be tied up with their jobs. When Malcolm lost his, it's like he lost a part of himself."

"I'm guessing the job search has been pretty discouraging, then."

Mellie nodded. "At first Malcolm was treating finding a job like *having* a job. He was very organized. He made his resume really spiffy, created a list of jobs that seemed to fit what he could do, and arranged for interviews and follow-up calls. But as time went by and nothing came through, he started to really doubt himself. He started putting less time into looking for a job." Mellie shrugged. "Even worse, he started drinking more to deal with what was happening."

"I'm so sorry," Beatrice said again.

"That's why I didn't want Georgia coming over when she was going to show me how to set up my website. I was embarrassed by Malcolm. I feel awful saying that, but it's true. I know I need to be supporting him now and trying to help him get through this awful time but it's tough to do. I wish he could see that what he's doing is just making everything worse." She sighed. "Now it looks like I may be coming into a little money from Dad's estate. I'm not going to say the money won't help, especially since we've really run through everything in our savings account. But I also can't think of it as a band-aid. Money will help with some of our problems, but not others."

Beatrice hesitated. She'd kept thinking about what Edgenora had said about Mellie and Shirley arguing the day Shirley died. Edgenora had said she'd tell Ramsay and she was so organized and focused that Beatrice had no doubt she would—and likely in an expedient manner. But maybe there was some sort of reasonable explanation for the argument.

"Mellie, I know you said you didn't know Shirley," started Beatrice slowly. "You mentioned that you'd never met her."

But Beatrice couldn't continue any further because, to her consternation, Mellie suddenly burst into tears.

Beatrice stood up and hurried over to give Mellie a hug and a tissue from the packet in her purse.

"I'm sorry," murmured Beatrice as Mellie blew her nose with enthusiasm. "I know you're going through such a tough time right now."

"No, no," said Mellie, her voice cracking. "It's just that I feel so bad about having lied—to you and to everybody else."

Beatrice just stood there quietly, waiting for Mellie to continue in her own time. Mellie blew her nose again and said in a soft voice that Beatrice had to strain to hear, "I just felt bad for my mom, that's all."

"Of course you did," said Beatrice. "I'm sure it must have been very hard for her to have Shirley trying to contact the family."

Mellie nodded, still not meeting Beatrice's gaze. "It really was. Mom doesn't show it the way other people do. She's learned to bury her hurt. Actually, I think she's learned to bury most of her feelings."

Beatrice remembered that Jack had said very much the same thing. It was why Jack tried to take his mother to lunch—to get her out of what he perceived as an unhealthy environment for Tilda.

Mellie continued, "Jack had told me he was going over to talk with Shirley. But I knew he was really mad at her for continuing to try to contact the family. Between Laura and Shirley, Mom kept getting quieter and paler."

"I'm sure Jack is very protective of his mother. You probably are, too," said Beatrice.

"I am. But Jack wasn't just feeling protective of Mom. He was also worried because he heard Shirley was trying to get some sort of share of my dad's estate. Jack isn't someone who is greedy in any way, but he's lived a pretty meager existence for a while. I knew the idea of having Shirley going after the estate was upsetting to him. So I volunteered to go over and talk to Shirley instead."

Beatrice said, "That makes sense. You were probably worried that Jack was going to blow up at Shirley over the money."

"Exactly. Even though Jack is a pretty even-keeled guy, he can have a quick temper. Of course, ironically, *I* was the one who ended up blowing up at Shirley," said Mellie ruefully.

"What happened?" asked Beatrice.

Mellie took a deep breath and brushed a tear off her cheek. "I don't even really know. One minute I felt like we were having a perfectly reasonable adult conversation with each other. The next minute, I was screaming like a banshee at her."

She looked so dejected that Beatrice put a hand on her shoulder. "I'm guessing Shirley had something to do with the change. You don't exactly run around town yelling at people without cause."

Mellie gave her a grateful smile. "Thanks, Beatrice. I guess Shirley did have a hand in my reaction, although it's hard to think of that now that she's gone. Now I just feel so guilty about it. I feel like I made her have this really awful day and it ended up being the last day of her life."

"Yes, but you didn't know that at the time. Why would you? You need to let that go. At the time, it was just a day like any other."

Mellie nodded. "True." She took a deep breath. "Anyway, Shirley was absolutely delighted to see me at her door. She'd been trying to reach the family for days and then suddenly, there I was on her front porch."

"Did she invite you in?"

Mellie shook her head. "No. Which was fine . . . I wasn't planning on being there long. All I was going to do was to ask her to please stop trying to reach Mom. And Archibald had said that if she had any issues with Dad's will, she needed to address them through the courts, so I was going to tell her that, too. But mostly, I wanted to let her know that it was really stressful for Mom to have her calling all the time."

"Was your mother taking her calls?" Beatrice couldn't imagine Tilda was.

"No. But the calls were stressful, all the same. Anyway, Shirley's lip curled and she said that she had absolutely no intention of letting up with the phone calls. That it didn't bother her one bit if Tilda was inconvenienced by them."

Mellie's face flushed even brighter at the memory.

"Did she say why?" asked Beatrice. "That seems really unreasonable."

"Yeah. She said it was because she needed money *right then*. She didn't want to wait for money to go through the courts because she had a mortgage to pay. Shirley said Dad had left her high and dry and she was going into debt because of it." Mellie's mouth twisted unhappily.

Beatrice was quiet at this, not wanting to say anything that would make Mellie even more unhappy than she already was.

Mellie continued, "That's what made me go totally off the rails. Shirley was acting as if the house that Dad had provided for her was *our* problem. The family's. That just made me go completely berserk. I mean, having another woman put up in a nice house was already quite a slap in the face to my mother. But making her pick up the tab for it after my father died was something else."

"And that's what you told her," Beatrice said, nodding.

"Yes. Although I could have chosen a quieter tone and a nicer way of putting it." Mellie's face was rueful. "I've been feeling really guilty about how I talked to her. Plus, I should have picked up on the fact that she wasn't exactly listening to me when I was yelling at her. When I used a quieter tone of voice, she actually seemed to be paying attention to what I was saying. When I was screaming, she totally tuned me out." Mellie gave a short laugh. "Which makes total sense. I'd tune out, too, if someone was bellowing at me on my own front porch." She looked over at Beatrice. "But I know I lied about having met Shirley. I feel bad about that, too—I don't usually make a habit of lying to my friends and you've been so kind, Beatrice."

Beatrice made a dismissive gesture. "That's the last thing you should be worrying about, Mellie."

"No, I *am* worried about it. That's not how I treat my friends. My friends are how I'm making it through all this mess. I just felt so guilty about how I spoke to Shirley that I didn't want anyone else to know. Although obviously someone found out." She gave an unhappy laugh again. "Small towns."

Beatrice was careful not to mention that Edgenora had been Shirley's neighbor and Beatrice's informant. "That's completely understandable."

Mellie sighed. "It wasn't just that, though. I also didn't want Ramsay and the state police to know I'd been at Shirley's house, yelling at her, the day she died. I had the feeling that might be regarded as somewhat suspicious."

"Well, obviously she was fine when you left her," said Beatrice.

Mellie nodded. "And it wasn't as if anyone had arrived at the house when I was leaving. If I'd had any useful information to give the police, I'd have given it to them."

Mellie seemed to want to be quiet then, resuming her work inside the desk, so Beatrice delved back into clearing out files, the upbeat music striking an odd note in such an oppressive environment.

After another fifteen minutes passed, Mellie abruptly turned off the music, frowning. "What is—I don't understand what this is."

Chapter Fifteen

B eatrice stretched her cramped legs a little before standing up. "Is something wrong?"

"Maybe. Yeah, I definitely think so."

Mellie held out a piece of paper and what looked like a couple of photographs that had been blown up. Beatrice walked over to Lester's desk and carefully peered over Mellie's shoulder.

"This was in that secret compartment I told you about," she said slowly. "So I guess the police wouldn't have found it when they were searching my dad's office."

The piece of paper was some sort of report on what appeared to be an accident. Beatrice frowned as she read. The details of a vehicle were listed, the location, and the time. She studied the photo next and saw Jack Dawson with wide, staring eyes. "Is this a police report?"

Mellie shook her head. "No, I don't think so. On the second page, there's the name of some kind of private investigator business. And that's Jack in those pictures."

"Jack was involved in an accident?"

"Not as far as I knew, but he must have been, according to that report. Beatrice, it sounds like a pedestrian was really hurt."

Beatrice's brow crinkled as she quickly read through the entire document. Sure enough, the report detailed the injuries a pedestrian had sustained. Plus, even more worrying, Jack had apparently left the scene. It was a hit-and-run. She looked at Mellie and handed her the documents and photos. "What are you going to do?"

Mellie's eyes were huge. "This looks really bad, doesn't it? I don't think this was reported to the police at all."

"I don't totally understand what this was. Why would a private investigator have this kind of information? How did he happen to be there? Was he blackmailing your father to keep the report quiet?"

Mellie shook her head slowly. "This wasn't the first time my dad hired a private investigator. He liked to know the background of people he did business with—he mentioned in the past that it gave him a psychological leverage, even if he never used the information. He must have also been keeping tabs on his own family sometimes." She looked a little sick.

Beatrice remembered during her conversation with Jack that he'd thrown in a bit about private investigators.

"Why would your dad have had someone following Jack?"

Mellie gave a short laugh. "Maybe because Jack was always trying to get money from Dad? He could have wanted to find out how Jack was spending it. I guess he thought he was using drugs or something."

"Was he?"

"No. Definitely not. I mean, Jack likes his whiskey, but so did my father. Whatever money my dad gave him went to living expenses. Delivery truck drivers don't make a ton, you know." She covered her mouth. "Ohhh. What am I going to do?"

Beatrice hesitated. "You could tell Ramsay about what you've found. Let him decide how important it is."

Mellie immediately shook her head. "I don't know if I can do that, Beatrice. I've always gotten along with Jack really well—he's the only one who's ever really added some lightness to family occasions. We'll all be sitting at the table, gloomy and uncomfortable, and Jack will come in and make us all smile. Well, make *most* of us smile, anyway. My dad and Archibald made for a tough crowd. Jack's my baby brother." She shook her head again. "No. I'll talk to my mother about it first. Although it's going to break her heart to hear about it."

"That's quite a burden to bear on your shoulders," said Beatrice. She was also thinking it was too big a burden for *her* shoulders. It made her complicit in covering up a crime, from what she understood. Jack was involved in a hit-and-run. From all appearances, his victim had suffered some terrible injuries. The police should certainly be involved, even if it wasn't connected to Lester's death.

It apparently hadn't yet occurred to Mellie that Beatrice might not feel the same way Mellie did about concealing the information about Jack. "I'll share the burden with my mother. I'm sure Jack didn't have anything to do with my father's death. He couldn't have. He's not the one with the temper, you know. To me, it seems that whoever lashed out at my father had done it in a rage." Her eyes stared blankly around the room where her father had died, as if imagining the scene.

Now Beatrice was feeling especially uncomfortable. She was happy to give Mellie a hand with her father's things but didn't like what she felt she was getting pulled into. Family secrets? Private investigators? Crimes that were covered up? She felt the sudden need to leave the house and head back to her small cottage for a cuddle with Noo-noo and a cup of herbal tea. But she'd told Mellie she would help her out.

Beatrice took a deep breath. "Mellie, maybe we should just keep working on weeding out things in the office."

She saw a look of hurt pass over Mellie's features and quickly added, "It's just that I'm not feeling really comfortable about you not going to Ramsay about this. I'm happy to help you out with the office, but let's focus on that for right now."

Mellie shook her head. "I'm sorry, Beatrice. I didn't mean to pull you into anything. And I really appreciate you giving me a hand with all this stuff. But right now I'm not feeling up to this. I've just got too much on my mind."

Beatrice stood up, feeling relieved. She couldn't wait to get out of that house. "I totally understand. I hate what you're having to go through."

Mellie said, "Oh, but the suits. There are so many of them and we didn't even get to Dad's closet. How about if I give you an armful of them and you can at least take a small load to the church clothes closet? I'm sorry—I should have started us in his room."

So Mellie and Beatrice walked out to Beatrice's car, each carrying a full armful of expensive suits. Mellie waved sadly at Beatrice as she pulled out of the driveway to head to the church.

Beatrice's mind was whirling. Part of her wanted to go straight to the police station and talk with Ramsay. Because she knew she was *definitely* going to tell him this, regardless of what Mellie would have her do. It was the right thing to do. She wanted to sort out in her head exactly how to tell him, though. For that, she needed a few minutes for her brain to process it all.

When she pulled up to the church, she saw a delivery truck there. She slowly got out of her car just as Jack left the church. Looking at him, she noticed a huge change in his demeanor from the last time she'd seen him. She wondered if it was just because she knew more about him now or if he'd actually changed. Jack had been so cheerful and carefree when she'd encountered him at the Patchwork Cottage when she'd been there with Will.

He smiled at her as she came up. "Hi there. No sidekick with you today?"

"No, I'm sadly baby-free," said Beatrice with a return smile. "How are you holding up?"

Jack looked serious again, just as he had when she'd first seen him. "It's nice of you to ask. I was just wondering if I might possibly sit in the chapel here for a few minutes. I just finished my delivery for the church and my break is about to start. Do you know if it's open?"

"It's always open, actually, and it's a great place to sit and think." Beatrice paused. "Wyatt might also be available if you'd like to speak with him. Sometimes talking to someone can really help."

Jack nodded. "He's good to talk to. I did look for him when I was in the church, but he was in some sort of meeting with a bunch of church officials."

"Oh, that's right. He has his regular meeting with the elders and deacons now. Tell you what—I'll text and ask him to head to the chapel when he's done and see if you're still there."

"Thank you," he said quietly. Then he hesitated, looking as if he wanted to say something else, but wasn't quite sure how to put it. He was so different from the way he'd been before.

Beatrice said, "I'm no Wyatt, but I'd be happy to speak with you, too. If you need an ear."

She wasn't sure Jack would take her up on it but was surprised to see his eyes light up. "That would be great. I'm sorry, though, aren't I taking you away from what you're supposed to be doing here?"

"I'm just dropping off items for the clothes closet, but I can do that later. I left them in the trunk once I saw you. You looked as if you had something on your mind."

Jack said, "Definitely. There's so much on my mind that I'm having a tough time sleeping at night. How about if I give you a hand with the clothes closet stuff and you can walk with me to the chapel?"

When Beatrice opened the trunk, she started to warn Jack of the contents when Jack immediately took a sharp breath. "Ah. I think I recognize these particular garments."

"I'm sorry, I should have given you more of a heads-up."

"No, it's fine. I'm really glad you're giving them to the church. It makes me feel like some sort of good might come out of them." Jack's mouth curved up at one end. "Lester wasn't one for charity. I don't think he gave a cent away to anyone in his entire life. I like the idea that someone might be able to get a job or attend their wedding in his suits."

He picked up the bulk of them, still on hangers, as Beatrice shut the trunk. They headed to the clothes closet where Jack carefully hung them up, dusting lint from a couple of the jackets. Then they walked to the chapel.

Beatrice had always loved the little chapel. She was secretly a bit fonder of it than she was of the large sanctuary. The chapel had gleaming wooden pews, a lush carpet, and beautiful stone walls with small stained-glass windows. It was always quiet in there and was the perfect place for prayer or meditation. The entire room had a very calming, soothing effect.

They sat in one of the pews and Jack said, "This is exactly what I needed. This space."

"It's beautiful in here, isn't it?"

Jack nodded. "It makes me feel like everything is all right. That everything will work out."

"Yes. Sometimes it's hard to see that things will get better. But they usually do."

Jack turned to look at her. "Do you really think that? Even for those of us who are a little less than perfect?"

"Absolutely."

Jack nodded again and looked back toward the front of the chapel. "You know, I've done a lot of sinning in my life. I'm really feeling the effects of it now."

Beatrice wanted to bring up the fact that she already knew about the hit-and-run, but was afraid it would put Mellie in a bad position. Jack would surely ask how she knew about it, and she'd have to mention their office decluttering and what Mellie had found. Better to have Jack tell her about it himself . . . if he would. So she just looked attentively at him.

"With all the tragedies going on, I guess it's caused me to reflect on my own life. I definitely want to make some changes. Whenever I think about my life, it just makes me feel bad . . . remorseful, I guess is the word."

"You can do it," said Beatrice quickly. "Reflecting and regretting the things you've done and the people you've hurt along the way is a great first step."

Jack was quiet for a moment, looking toward the front of the chapel again. Then he said, "Shirley's death is another thing I feel bad about. I guess it's mostly me feeling guilty because it was such a relief when I found out she was gone. That's another reason I'm here. All Shirley was doing was dumping more stress on top of us by making demands." He quickly added, "Like I told the cops, though, I didn't have anything to do with her death. I was just glad it happened. I was actually at home when she died, which is pretty unusual."

"Where are you usually?"

Jack gave a short laugh. "I'm usually at bars in Lenoir. That's something else I think I need to change. Dappled Hills doesn't really have places to hang out and drink so I'm driving all the way back and forth to Lenoir to do it. That means I'm on the road after I've had a few. Plus, I'm just not the best guy when I've been drinking. I turn into a different person. Ironically, if I *had* been out drinking, I'd have a hope of an alibi for Shirley's death. But I was home trying to get some sleep."

Beatrice thought that insomnia seemed to be a common thread for the family. "Did you know Shirley?"

Jack shook his head. "I'm not going to say I *knew* her. But I did go to her house the day before she died."

Beatrice just quietly nodded even though she felt this was a startling revelation. She wondered if Ramsay was aware of Jack having been there. And, clearly, Mellie hadn't realized it. That was the whole reason she'd gone over to Shirley's herself—she'd been worried about Jack blowing his top over there.

"I just felt like she was being very pushy for money. I mean, if anyone understands needing cash, it's me. But the whole family is being put through the wringer and having Shirley making all these demands was creating even more stress for my mom. And Mom was stressed enough as it was."

Beatrice asked, "She was in contact with the family a lot?"

Jack snorted. "I think she called every single last one of us. She insisted Lester had written her into his will and had given her something. She told me she was in a spot because he had been the one paying for her house. I felt bad for her but told her that she was just going to have to do what I've been doing—work for it. Lester wasn't exactly giving me a lot of handouts, either. I got a job, at *least* a job—sometimes two, and made money that way. It's not fun but it's a lot better than worrying about having a place to live."

Beatrice said, "You don't think your father left Shirley anything in his will, then?"

"Not a dime. I've seen the will. I told her she should find some other old guy to date." He shook his head. "I feel guilty about the way I spoke to her, especially now that she's gone."

They were quiet for a few moments, allowing the peace of the chapel to lend its soothing air.

Beatrice finally said, "Do you have any thoughts about who could be responsible?"

Jack hesitated, looking miserable. He shrugged. "Maybe Laura was involved. Maybe she just got carried away when my father wouldn't help her financially. I could totally see that—it made me furious when he wouldn't give me a hand with money. Laura could have flown into a rage and lashed out at him. Shirley could have found out and blackmailed Laura. That makes the most sense to me. We know Shirley needed the money and we know she was on the property the morning Lester died." Jack shrugged. "I know it couldn't have been my family involved in this. I hope Ramsay and they are looking in the right place. They're asking me a ton of questions because of the fact I always need money. What they don't get is that needing money is a chronic condition for me. It's not something I'd kill over."

The door opened behind us, and Wyatt came in. Beatrice stood up and gave Wyatt's hand a squeeze. "I'll leave you two since I know Jack's breaktime is probably limited."

Jack smiled at her. "Thanks, Beatrice. For everything."

Chapter Sixteen

B eatrice left the church, mulling over what Jack had said. Then she looked at her watch, thinking it might be good to check in with Piper. When she called there, Ash picked up Piper's phone. "Hey Beatrice," he said in a low voice.

"Is everything okay over there?" she asked.

"It is. I came home early today from work to help out. Piper didn't sleep great last night and is finally taking a nap, but Will has gobs of energy for some reason," said Ash wryly.

"How about if I collect Will for some grandmama time? That way Piper can nap, and you can get things done there."

"Would you?" asked Ash, sounding relieved. "That would be a huge help."

"I'll be right there."

Will was as adorable as ever when Beatrice walked in, but he was definitely wired. He rushed over and gave Beatrice a big hug and she hugged him back.

Ash said in a low voice, "Sure this is okay, Beatrice? He's a pistol right now."

"Perfect for some outdoor time. We had such a fun time at the park playground recently that we'll head back over there."

Ash nodded. "Good idea. Just run him back by the house whenever you need a break."

"I'll be just fine. I seem to shed a few years when I'm with my grandson, so I can keep up with him better. Anyway, let's let poor Piper get a good nap in."

Will and Beatrice left hand-in-hand. Beatrice drove them over to the park. "What are you going to play on today, Will? Swings? Slides? The sandbox?"

Will gave an enthusiastic but entirely indecipherable answer. Beatrice said, "Well, that sounds like fun."

She was helping Will out of his car seat when she heard someone calling her name in an imperative way. Looking up, she saw Miss Sissy bounding across the street from the Patchwork Cottage.

Beatrice sighed. She wasn't at all sure she had the energy to keep up with Will *and* Miss Sissy. But perhaps Miss Sissy would be in a useful sort of mood.

"Did you spot us from the shop window, Miss Sissy?" asked Beatrice lightly as the old woman gave Will a big hug.

"Saw the car," she noted with a shrug of her slender shoulder. Then she and Will skipped off to the swings. It was good to see that Miss Sissy was as energetic as ever and seemed more than able to match Will's energy level.

Two adults were definitely not needed to supervise the baby swing, so Beatrice sat down on a nearby park bench to watch as Will lifted his face and smiled every time the swing was in forward motion. His wispy baby hair blew in the breeze. Beatrice was so caught up in admiring her grandchild that she didn't notice someone jogging on the park trail until her name was once again called.

"Oh, Laura," said Beatrice. She smiled at the young woman. "This is a great trail, isn't it? I guess you've figured out that it connects to one of the big trailheads up the mountain?"

"I did, but it took me a while. Honestly, this is a great town," said Laura, sitting down next to Beatrice.

Miss Sissy looked askance at Laura, scowling at her on the bench. Beatrice couldn't tell if that was because the old woman knew something about Laura or if it was simply because she was concerned about sharing Will with someone else.

"Are you thinking about making a move here?" asked Beatrice. Ordinarily, that wouldn't have surprised her. Dappled Hills was a gorgeous mountain village with all sorts of amenities. But Laura's family hadn't exactly put out the welcome mat for her.

Laura knit her brows and Beatrice had the feeling she was thinking the same thing. "Maybe. I hadn't thought about that at all, but I'm starting to really enjoy it here. I'd figured I'd head back home, but then I realized there's nothing left for me there now that my mom's gone. Dappled Hills has everything I love. The only thing would be finding a job here."

"What is your line of work?"

Laura gave her a rueful look. "That's a good question. It's really anything I can line up. Usually I work in some sort of hospitality job. But I'm hoping to save enough money to pay for some extra schooling. I'd love to become a nurse one day. I was always really interested in science, but my mother didn't have the money to pay for me to go to school."

Will called out to Beatrice and she smiled and waved at him as he grinned at her from the swing.

Miss Sissy intoned, "Poppycock!" glaring at Laura the whole time.

Laura looked startled by this pronouncement and Beatrice said quietly, "Miss Sissy is something of a local character. That's my grandson in the swing and she's giving me a hand with him today."

Laura seemed to accept this explanation although she gave Miss Sissy a wary look.

Beatrice continued, "One thing you could do is to commute over to Lenoir. It's a pretty drive and there isn't much traffic. There would be a lot more hospitality-related jobs over there."

"Thanks! I'll take a look. I still have hopes of developing a relationship with at least one of my half-siblings and moving here would be the easiest way to make that happen." There was a wistful look on Laura's face that made Beatrice sad.

Laura added, "I'm taking up jogging again to help me out with some stress relief. It's good for general health, too. I came to the realization that what I'm doing here in Dappled Hills may or may not be helpful—for me or for the family."

"Getting to that point of realization must have taken time."

"It did. Mostly, I've been awake at night thinking about it," said Laura wryly.

Beatrice again saw the common thread of sleeplessness among the Dawson clan, even to the extended members.

Laura continued, "One of the problems is that I'm causing the family pain, just by the sheer fact of my existence. You know? Sort of like Shirley. I'm just walking, talking evidence of

Lester's infidelity. If I do stay here in Dappled Hills, I'll avoid the family completely. They need to be the ones to reach out to me instead of the other way around."

Beatrice nodded but wondered if Laura understood how very difficult it could be to avoid the family in a town the size of Dappled Hills. You continuously run into people you want to see as well as people you'd rather not.

Miss Sissy hissed, "Evillll."

Laura stared at her in consternation and Beatrice put Miss Sissy temporarily in the column of people she'd rather not run into. "Don't worry about her," she said to Laura. Laura looked as if she'd lost her train of thought and Beatrice prompted, "You were going to keep away from the family?"

"That's right. Maybe that will end up being a way to earn their trust. Maybe we can end up forging some sort of relationship in the end."

Beatrice asked, "Are you planning on giving up your claim to your father's estate, then?"

Laura shook her head. "I've been speaking to an attorney. Quite an expensive activity, speaking with attorneys, by the way. Anyway, I think going through a lawyer is the best way to handle things. The family has done nothing to me. It's not their fault that I've felt unacknowledged and marginalized. Addressing it impersonally, through the courts, is the best way to handle things."

"That sounds like a smart approach."

The two of them sat on the bench watching as Will pointed over to the sandbox. Miss Sissy stopped the swing and Beatrice rose to help her take Will out of the swing. The old woman scowled at her and Beatrice quickly sat down again.

"She's fierce," said Laura. Her voice held both trepidation and admiration.

"Isn't she? But she can be very sweet, too."

Laura gave Miss Sissy a doubtful look. They were quiet for a few moments and then Laura said, "I may need to retain an attorney for other reasons, too. The police have been speaking with me again. They seem to think I might have had something to do with Shirley's death."

"I'm sure that's just police protocol to re-interview everyone." Beatrice watched as Will happily pushed the sand into a pile in the sandbox so that a toy truck could pick it up.

"You may be right," allowed Laura, "But the fact of the matter is, they think there's a connection there. They seem hung up on the fact that I don't have an alibi. But how on earth could I have *gotten* one? I don't know anyone in town to speak of, so it's not like I'm hanging out with people. I'm not married, so I don't have anyone to say I was tucked away in my hotel all night. It's frustrating. I was asleep, but there's no one to vouch for that."

Beatrice said, "I know it's frustrating and very worrisome. Just know that Ramsay is always a very fair man and is good at his job. I'm sure he's just doing what he's supposed to do in order to cover the bases and perform a complete investigation."

Laura nodded, looking a little relieved. "Okay. Good to hear he's fair. This whole experience has been sort of surreal to me. Not to mention, very disappointing. The main reason I came over here was to connect with my father and establish some sort of relationship with him. That was the very first disappointment—being completely rejected by him. The next was his passing and knowing that I'd never be able to form that connection at all. Then the family's rejection of me came next. The lack of financial provisions in my father's will is another blow, but it was by far the smallest."

"How did your mother meet your father? Did you live here for a time?"

Laura shook her head. "My father's company had an office in my mother's town. It was a rural area in North Carolina that he had a factory in. He met her on one of his trips there to oversee the factory. Once he realized I was on the way, he basically cut her off." Laura's lips tightened as she thought about it.

"That must have been incredibly stressful for your mother. What did she do?"

Laura said, "She moved back in with her parents, and they helped her out by giving her a hand with raising me. That's where I grew up—a town where nothing really happened."

Laura fell quiet again and they watched as Will and Miss Sissy played with trucks in the sandbox. Then Laura said, "I wonder if Shirley came from the same kind of background. She could have, you know. I have the feeling she and I might have had a good deal in common. I feel sorry for her, too, because my father treated her just about as poorly as he treated me, from what I understand."

"Did you talk to Shirley?" asked Beatrice with surprise.

A brief look of consternation crossed Laura's features. She hesitated and then said, "Briefly, yes. Shirley sought me out. I think she had some sort of idea to join forces and approach the family together—a kind of show of force."

"I'm guessing that wasn't very appealing to you."

Laura shook her head. "Definitely not. I was already coming across too strong and realizing I needed to rein myself in. I'm not going to just show up at the house anymore, for instance. And they won't take my calls, so I guess I'll just let my attorney do my talking for me." She looked momentarily dejected again before continuing. "Anyway, I did feel bad for Shirley. She was just as pushy as I was, I guess. But it's hard when there's something you want and it seems like there are gatekeepers. Unlike me, Shirley never realized she needed to back off a little."

"Do you think that might have been what got her killed?" Beatrice shivered a little as a cool breeze blew against them.

"Maybe. I don't really know. The whole family had good reason to want to get rid of Shirley. She was definitely making a nuisance of herself. Money is a great motivator. Of course, I don't know the family at all so I can't say who is more likely to have done something like that."

Beatrice said, "You seem like you're in a better place than when I saw you at the Dawson house."

"Well, exercise has helped me sort my head out," said Laura ruefully. "Otherwise, things tend to fester. It *is* a lot of stress to constantly make demands, even if the demands are reasonable. It doesn't help that the police believe I could somehow be involved in these deaths."

Beatrice said, "Jogging sounds like a great way to help reduce all that stress. I know you don't really know anyone in town—let me be an ear for you if you need someone to talk to. Plus, my husband is the minster of the Presbyterian church and he's an excellent listener." She jotted down their phone numbers on a piece of paper she found in her purse. As an afterthought, she also wrote down their address.

"Thanks for this," said Laura. There was genuine relief and gratitude in her voice. "I feel like I've been rejected by everyone since I arrived in town. This means a lot."

Beatrice said, "I'm happy to help. I wrote down our address, too. You're welcome to stop by, of course. You might enjoy extending your jog through our neighborhood, too. We connect straight to downtown and it's a quiet, nice area."

"That sounds great." She glanced at her watch. "I'd better get back to it. Thanks again."

Chapter Seventeen

After she left, Beatrice joined Miss Sissy and Will in the sandbox. Will was getting increasingly enthusiastic with the trucks, and sand started flying around in a rather alarming way. After Will got some in his mouth, Beatrice decided it was perhaps time to find another area of the playground to play in.

Which was precisely when Ash called her. "Piper is all finished with her nap and says she feels terrific."

"Does she? That's great news! Would you like me to keep Will with me for a little while?"

"If you don't mind, could you bring him back home? She says she's really missed him while she's been sick," said Ash.

"Absolutely. Just a heads-up that he might be a little sandy."

Ash chuckled. "That's just proof he's had an excellent time with his grandmother."

After they hung up, Beatrice tried to round up Will and Miss Sissy. It was difficult to do, mostly because of Miss Sissy, who was grumbling under her breath and dragging her feet.

"We'll come to the park another time," promised Beatrice.

More grumbling commenced.

"Are you heading back to the Patchwork Cottage, or would you like me to drop you by your house?" asked Beatrice, pretending the grumbling wasn't happening.

Miss Sissy considered this. Likely figuring she'd have a smidgeon more time with Will if she stuck with them, she picked being dropped off by her house.

They finally climbed into Beatrice's car, Miss Sissy choosing to sit in the backseat with Will, which made Beatrice feel like a chauffeur. As she set off to take the old woman back home, she asked, "Did you know the young woman who was talking to me at the park? Laura?"

Miss Sissy made a hissing sound from the back which Beatrice took as an affirmation. "Why don't you like her?"

"Saw her with Lester in downtown." Miss Sissy muttered this in such a low voice that Beatrice had to strain to hear her.

"Lester was her *father*. She was trying to establish a relationship with him," explained Beatrice helpfully.

Miss Sissy was quiet at this revelation.

"So did you know Lester, then?"

Miss Sissy growled, "Went to school with me."

"*Really*?" Beatrice now was quiet herself as she tried to figure this out. It all made sense, actually. He had been a very old man . . . certainly old enough to be a contemporary of Miss Sissy's. But Miss Sissy seemed especially ancient to Beatrice.

"I was a senior when he was a freshman," she said offhandedly.

Beatrice said, "I'm surprised that boys and girls were in the same high school when you were in school."

Looking in her rearview mirror, she saw Miss Sissy glare at her. "We were!"

Beatrice supposed the county likely didn't have the funds at the time for two separate schools. "What was he like back then? Was he always wealthy?"

"Poor."

Beatrice said, "Oh, so he was a self-made man."

"Hard and mean. Ambitious."

That was another way of putting it, Beatrice supposed. "What made him so mean?"

"Other kids. They gave him a hard time. He got rich and came back to show them."

Beatrice said, "Ah. So he was bullied and that motivated him."

Miss Sissy apparently had said all she wanted to say on the subject and was pointing out animals to Will in one of his picture books.

After she'd dropped the old woman back home, Beatrice headed over to Piper and Ash's house.

"Mama," said Will as they pulled up into the driveway.

"Yes, indeed! Are you excited to see your Mama? She's excited to see *you*."

Will nodded solemnly. "Sick."

"Yes, she has been sick, hasn't she? But she's feeling much better now."

Beatrice extricated Will from his car seat and headed to the front door with him. Ash opened the door and Will went bounding off inside to find Piper.

"Can you come in for a minute?" asked Ash. "If you've been at the park, wouldn't you like a glass of water?"

Beatrice suddenly realized that she *was* rather thirsty. "Actually, that would be great."

She walked into their sunny living room where Piper, looking much more like herself, was ensconced on the sofa with Will. "Thanks for all your help, Mama."

"Oh, it was my pleasure. You know how much I love spending time with Will. I'm just glad you're feeling better."

Ash came in to join them with a glass of water for Beatrice.

She took a big sip of it and then said, "Ash, I was wondering if you knew Jack Dawson."

Ash said with a laugh, "That's a name from the past. Are you doing a little investigating, maybe?"

"Just keeping my ear out, that's all," said Beatrice, trying to sound convincing since Piper was looking a little worried about the idea of her mother doing any investigating.

"Sure, I knew him. Mom wasn't happy about me hanging out with him, though, so we kind of went our separate ways at some point in high school. She thought he was trouble."

Beatrice could certainly see that. Jack had trouble written all over him, as charming as he was.

"Mom thought he might be a bad influence on me. He was one of those kids who got bored easily and hated doing schoolwork. He'd ditch class and hop in his car and head off to the beach on a whim."

"The *beach*? That's hours away."

Ash nodded. "Exactly. That's the kind of thing he'd do on a regular basis. Anyway, we stopped being in touch the last couple of years that we were in school together. A lot of it was because we were hanging out with different people but some of it was because Mom wasn't crazy about him."

"Makes sense." Beatrice turned to Piper and gave her a smile. "Your color looks so much better than it did. Are you feeling any stronger?"

"*So* much better. Thanks so much to you, Meadow, and Ash for helping me out. I'm all better now and ready for life to go back to normal."

"Whatever normal means," said Beatrice dryly. "It's been a little on the weird side lately."

Will bounced off to go get a toy and Piper said, "How are things going with Ramsay's investigation?"

"Well, there haven't been any arrests yet, at least as far as I know. There are a couple of things I need to fill in Ramsay about that I've gathered."

Piper quirked an eyebrow. "How diligent has your gathering been?"

"Oh, very casual. You know how it is in Dappled Hills. You just hear about things."

Piper nodded. "I'm sure people aren't quite as open talking with Ramsay as they are with you."

Beatrice pulled her phone out. "While I'm thinking about it, I'm going to ask him to run by on his way home so I can give him a full report." She typed up a text message and said, "And now I'm going to get out of your hair so you can play with Will for a little while. I think he's excited about it."

Will had run back into the living room with a toy car that drove itself at the flip of a switch.

"Thanks again, Mama," said Piper as Beatrice let herself out the door.

Back home, she decided to work on her latest quilting project while waiting for Ramsay to come by. She was trying to get rid of some of the extra fabric in her stash. She had a variety of fat quarters and some solid yard pieces which she was turning into an over-the-shoulder quilted bag and a reversible bucket that Will could use to put some of his toys in. Judging from the number of toys he received from his doting grandmothers, Beatrice acknowledged that he might need several buckets.

There was a tap on the door and Beatrice put down the fabric she was working on. Noo-noo gave excited barks. Beatrice fully expected to see Ramsay when she opened the door, but instead it was Laura standing there.

Laura's face was slightly flushed, and she was wearing her jogging clothes. She glanced behind Beatrice to see the fabric spread on the table and said apologetically, "I'm sorry—it looks like you're in the middle of something."

Beatrice shook her head quickly. "Oh, it's just some of my quilting. I was just filling in some quiet space. Would you like to come in?"

Laura hesitated and then, spotting Noo-noo's grinning face, laughed. "Sure. Just for a few minutes so I can let you get back to your quilting. I'd like the chance to visit with this little girl."

Beatrice led her inside and Laura immediately stooped down to get on the corgi's level. "What a sweetie."

"Can I get you some water? It looks like you've been jogging."

Laura said, "Actually, that would be amazing. And you were right about your neighborhood—it's a great place to jog in."

Beatrice fixed them both some tall glasses of ice water. Laura gave Noo-noo a few more rubs and then settled in a chair at the table with the little dog close to her leg. Laura looked at the bits of fabric on the table and said, "I wish I were good at crafts. Somehow, I can never seem to get measurements and things right. What are you making?"

Beatrice told her how she was using up the mishmash of fabrics that were scattered over the table in colorful cacophony.

"That sounds like a great way of using up materials. That's another thing that stops me from taking up a craft—not having any place to keep craft materials. Plus the cost of them," added Laura ruefully. Then she brightened. "Although that might be getting better soon. That's one reason I wanted to stop by and talk to you. My attorney reached out to the family's attorney, and they appear to be ready to make some concessions."

Beatrice smiled at her. "That's great! I'm sure that will really help you out in starting out a new chapter."

"Exactly. But I have even *better* news than that. Mellie gave me a call last night." Laura's face broke open with a huge grin.

"Really? That's wonderful!"

"Isn't it? I couldn't believe it when I heard her on the phone. At first, I thought maybe it was a call to ask me to leave the family alone. That's because I had a tough time hearing her on the phone. But her voice was so low because she was apologizing—she said she felt bad about the way the family had treated me, and she wanted to meet up with me for lunch!"

Beatrice gave her a hug. "That's fantastic, Laura. I know how much you wanted that to happen."

"Exactly. I grew up as an only child and then, when my mom passed, I just felt so completely alone in the world. Having a sister means everything to me. And Mellie seems like such a great person. What can you tell me about her? I'd like to ask all the right questions when we have lunch so there won't be any awkward silences. I really want it to be a *good* visit with each other."

Beatrice said, "Well, her big news is that she's starting her own business. She's launching a sort of quilt-on-demand online shop."

"So people give her their orders and then she makes a quilt according to their specs?"

Beatrice nodded. "That's what I understand. I'm guessing she'll have lots of gift quilts—for babies, weddings, that kind of thing."

Laura considered this for a moment before saying slowly, "It almost seems like Mellie has some of the same money troubles I do." She flushed a little and said, "I know that sounds silly, considering her family. But I drove by her house out of curiosity the other day and it seems like the kind of place I could afford more than the kind of home I'd think Mellie would live in."

"I don't think Lester was big into lending money," said Beatrice carefully. "And probably not giving it away, either. And Mellie's husband was laid off for a while so they've had some hard times."

"I see. That would make a big difference. Maybe Mellie and I have more in common than I thought." Laura paused and said, "I'm going to get out of your hair now, but could I use your restroom real quick before I go? All that water," she added ruefully.

"Of course you can." Beatrice pointed out the way to the bathroom.

As soon as Laura was in the restroom, the doorbell rang. Beatrice raised her eyebrows. She wasn't ordinarily so popular. When she opened the door, she saw Tilda standing there.

This was even more startling to Beatrice. "Hi Tilda," she said slowly.

Chapter Eighteen

Tilda gave her a tight smile. "I was wondering if I could talk to you for a few minutes. Is Wyatt here?"

"No, I'm afraid Wyatt is at the church right now. Please come on in. Is there something I can help you with?" Beatrice let Noo-noo into the backyard, thinking she might shed on Tilda's elegant outfit.

Tilda walked in. She was carrying a large tote bag from some expensive brand.

Beatrice was feeling a little leery about Laura coming out while Tilda was there. Things had been so peaceful when she'd been working on her quilt and now there was going to be all sorts of tension. It wasn't the way she'd envisioned her afternoon going.

"Won't you sit down? Can I get you anything to eat?"

Tilda shook her head impatiently, apparently as a reply to both questions. She immediately said, "You know about Jack, don't you?"

Beatrice hesitated. Tilda must have overheard her speaking with Mellie in the office about the pictures and the private investigator's report on Jack and the hit and run."

"Never mind. I can tell by your face that you do," said Tilda in a chilly voice. "There's something you need to know about Lester—he liked to control people. I think it drove him crazy that he couldn't control Jack. Jack has always been something of a free spirit." Tilda's cold demeanor softened for a few moments as she reflected on her son.

"I'm sorry," said Beatrice. "That must have been hard to witness as a mother."

Tilda shrugged. "It was just the way Lester operated. He decided to have a private investigator follow Jack because he couldn't figure out where Jack's money went." She gave a short laugh. "That's because Lester didn't understand how expensive it was to simply *live* these days. Jack had rent, utilities, and food. Those things cost a lot of money."

"Did Jack receive money from Lester?"

Tilda's mouth twisted. "He wouldn't give him a dime after a while. Just said he knew Jack was wasting it one way or another. He turned him down and then had him followed. That's how he knew about Jack's accident."

It seemed like Tilda's complete focus was Jack. There had been no mention of Jack's victim in the hit-and-run. Beatrice decided to bring it up.

"What happened to the victim?"

Tilda frowned. "Oh, Jack was all right. Shaken up, of course. And then that investigator gave Lester a report on the whole thing."

"No, I mean what happened to the person that Jack hit with the car."

Tilda's frown deepened. She shrugged. "The person was just fine. There was no real harm done. Lester even made a private donation to help the person with the medical bills from the hospital."

"That seems generous of Lester."

Tilda rolled her eyes a little. "He only did it because I demanded he do it. I didn't often interfere in things involving the children because Lester rarely listened to me and just did whatever he wanted to do. This time, he did what I asked. Anyway, Jack doesn't need to go to prison for this accident. The only reason it happened at all is because Lester sent the investigator to follow him."

Beatrice must have looked confused because Tilda impatiently elaborated. "Jack was trying to elude the investigator. It was a dark night and rainy outside. I'm not even sure where that pedestrian came from or why they were out in that weather at all. Jack sped up and tried to lose the person following him and accidentally ran into the pedestrian. An *accident*."

Beatrice said slowly, "This isn't all about the hit-and-run, is it? This is to do with Lester." She paused. "Jack murdered Lester, didn't he? Lester told Jack he had proof of the hit-and-run and was going to call the police?"

"I warned Lester," intoned Tilda. "I told him what would happen if he called the police. I'd walk out the door and never come back. I'd had enough through the years. Implicating our son in something criminal would be the final straw."

"But you said Lester rarely listened to you. This was one of the occasions when he didn't, wasn't it? He was planning to call Ramsay and tell him what happened."

Tilda's elegant features twisted into a smirk. "Lester suddenly had morals. Isn't that rich? He'd always been able to find the gray area in any ethical situation. But he said he couldn't possibly allow Jack to get away with something like the accident. Lester said it was his moral obligation to ensure Jack was punished for what he'd done. That's because Lester never liked Jack. Archibald was his favorite since they were so much more alike. Both of them were driven and ill-tempered."

Beatrice said slowly, "What I don't understand is why Lester didn't call the police right away if he was so worried about Jack's hit-and-run."

Tilda flinched a little at the phrase *hit-and-run*. It was clear she preferred the term *accident*. "Lester was like a cat with a mouse the whole last year. He enjoyed having the upper hand over Jack and used his knowledge to manipulate Jack—to keep him in order. If Jack asked for money, he would instantly remind him that he knew about the accident. Lester sort of milked the whole situation dry and then tired of it and told Jack he was going to turn him in."

"Why was Jack even over at your house to begin with? It was early in the day."

Tilda sighed and looked drained suddenly as her mind went back to that morning. "It was before work. Lester usually wasn't up that early, but he'd apparently overheard me speaking with Jack the night before. I was going to give him some cash before he headed off on the delivery truck. But since Lester had overheard us talking, he intercepted him and told him he wanted to speak with him in his office."

"So you *were* awake that morning."

Tilda gave me an irritated look. "Yes. But I wasn't in the office."

"I'm guessing that Lester told him he was finally done with Jack asking you or him for money. He was fed up enough that he decided to tell Jack he was going to tell Ramsay exactly who'd hit that pedestrian. What happened when Lester told Jack he was going to call the police? Did Jack lash out at his father? He was going to lose his freedom, after all. He must have felt desperate."

Tilda was silent, staring at Beatrice with those frosty eyes.

Beatrice continued, "Was it another accident? Did Jack never mean to kill his father? That briefcase was heavy, though. I hear Lester had it with him all the time and it was loaded with papers. And maybe Jack underestimated his strength. Because he must be pretty strong, right? He loads boxes all day for his delivery job."

Tilda seemed preoccupied with her tote bag for a moment before pulling a tire jack out.

Beatrice swallowed, but continued, "Shirley must have seen something the morning Lester died. Shirley had come over to the house to see where Lester was—and maybe to ask him for money for her mortgage payment. Did she spot Jack leaving the house? Was there something about Jack's demeanor that made her realize later what she'd witnessed?"

Tilda was silent, gripping the tire jack in a thin, veiny hand. Noo-noo, looking in through the window from the backyard, gave piercing barks, not liking what she was seeing.

Beatrice took a deep breath. "Shirley wouldn't have blackmailed Jack, though, would she? Jack didn't have any money. She'd have blackmailed *you*, Tilda. Shirley knew the last thing you'd want was to have your son go to jail for murder. You're the one who killed Shirley. Just like you are planning on killing me."

Tilda lunged for Beatrice, then stopped suddenly, her face incredulous as she saw Laura grimly standing in the doorway to the living room.

Laura raised her eyebrows at Tilda. "Really?"

Beatrice could have hugged her. But a loud knock on the door startled all three of them. Hesitantly, Beatrice headed for the door as Laura retrieved the tire iron from a sullen Tilda.

Beatrice was about to carefully look through the window to see who was there when the door flew open and Jack was there.

Tilda gave a wild cry and Laura said ominously, "Jack, we might be related, but I promise I'll take you out with this tire iron if you make one move."

Jack held his hands up, looking absolutely exhausted. "I don't want to hurt anyone. That's the last thing I want to do."

"Jack, what are you doing here?" asked his mother frantically. "You need to get away. Just get in your car and go. Don't even pack a bag."

"It's over, Mom," said Jack, giving Tilda a tired smile. "I told you I was going to turn myself in. Actually, I was going to give myself up for *both* murders since I didn't see any reason for both of us to go to prison."

"I wouldn't have let you. I *won't* let you," said Tilda fiercely.

"I don't exactly have a choice now, do I? I told you this didn't need to go any further. I was driving the delivery truck and saw your car outside. I figured what you might be up to." Jack looked grim.

Beatrice said quietly, "When we were in the chapel together, you looked so broken, Jack."

"Do I look better now?" he asked, giving Beatrice a smile.

She nodded. "Much. Tired, but not lost like you were looking before. You look like you have a purpose again."

He nodded. "You and Wyatt were both really helpful. I knew, deep inside, what I needed to do. I needed to confess to everything—the hit-and-run, Lester's death . . . I was even going to confess to Shirley's too, like I was saying. I did think I could protect Mom from having to go to jail, but I also *felt* responsible for Shirley's death."

Laura said, "It wouldn't have happened if you hadn't killed Lester."

"Right. My mom was just determined to protect me like the mama bear she is." He gave Tilda a wry grin, but Tilda was looking vacant again.

Beatrice picked up her phone and dialed Ramsay, briefly telling him what was going on.

Ramsay was there in minutes with the state police not far behind. He walked into the house to find Tilda, Laura, Jack, and Beatrice sitting in the living room as if engaged in a very quiet social visit. He took in the tire iron, still in Laura's hand, and Noo-noo sitting on Beatrice's lap and giving her comforting little licks on the neck.

"Tilda?" he asked.

Tilda's frostiness had melted and she now looked like a shadow of her former self as she slumped on Beatrice's sofa. She looked blankly at Ramsay.

Laura briskly said, "I saw the whole thing and heard it, too. Tilda was going to kill Beatrice for knowing too much."

Tilda momentarily roused from her vacant state long enough to give Laura a look of intense dislike.

Jack quickly said, "And I want to officially confess to my father's murder and the hit-and-run that happened almost a year ago."

A couple of state policemen came in the door. Ramsay motioned them over and then turned back to Tilda and Jack to read them their rights.

"Do either of you have anything to say about this?" Ramsay's voice, although stern, was not unkind.

Tilda's gaze swung up to meet his before sliding back down again. She gave an almost imperceptible shake of her head. Then, almost as an afterthought, she said, "Archibald."

"Archibald?" repeated Ramsay.

"He'll know what to do." Tilda sounded very sure of that.

Jack rolled his eyes. "Archibald *always* knows what to do."

Beatrice was sure he would. And that it would involve a good lawyer and advice to stay quiet and not say a word to the authorities. Unfortunately, even though Archibald seemed very image-conscious, there was not going to be any way to sweep this particular family situation under the carpet.

Since Tilda was clearly not in the mood to talk, one of the state policemen put her in handcuffs and took her outside to a police car.

"Would you like to speak with me about this now?" Ramsay asked Jack.

The exhaustion now looked even worse as Jack shook his head. "I'll wait until I'm down at the station if you don't mind. Thanks, Ramsay."

Ramsay looked pained. "I'm going to miss you at the writing and poetry club workshops."

Jack gave him a smile. "Hey, it's not all bad. I'll have plenty of time to be creative behind bars." One of the officers put him in handcuffs and led him out to a police car.

"Can you fill me in really quick?" asked Ramsay after she'd left. "Why did Tilda do this? Was it all about the money?"

Laura looked at Beatrice and Beatrice said, "No. It was about protecting Jack. I think Jack must be a favorite of Tilda's."

Ramsay was taking notes in his little notebook. "And Jack was responsible for—what?"

"That's what I wanted to speak with you about before things got crazy around here. When I was helping Mellie clean up her father's office, she found incriminating evidence against Jack."

Ramsay frowned. "In the office? But the state police searched the office after Lester's body was found there."

"There was a secret drawer, or compartment, or something that Mellie knew about. She said something about having played in that office when she'd been a child." Beatrice gave a slight shiver at the thought of the office. Only the imagination of a child could make the room into a fun place.

Ramsay picked up his pen again. "What kind of evidence did Mellie find?"

"Lester had disapproved of Jack asking him for money. According to Tilda, he was convinced that Jack was wasting it somehow . . . on drugs, or alcohol, or something like that. He hired a private investigator to follow Jack."

Laura shook her head. "Unbelievable."

Beatrice wondered if Laura was thinking that perhaps she hadn't missed out on very much by not having a relationship with her father.

Ramsay said, "Did Jack realize he was being tailed?"

"That's what I understand. He was apparently trying to shake the investigator when he accidentally hit a pedestrian."

Ramsay's eyebrows shot up. "Did he? There was a hit-and-run case that we never were able to find out any information on."

"Tilda was saying the victim wasn't really very hurt," said Beatrice dryly. "And that it was all okay because Lester helped out anonymously with the medical bills."

Ramsay snorted. "The victim had to learn to walk again. He'll never be the same."

"Tilda was just trying to justify Jack not turning himself in," said Laura.

"Clearly." Ramsay took a few more notes. "Okay. Jack was trying to get away from the investigator and hit the pedestrian. He drove off and the investigator did, too. Clearly, Lester was informed about what happened. So what was Lester doing with that information?"

"This happened a while back, I'm guessing?" asked Beatrice.

Ramsay considered this. "Well, not *that* long back. I'd say about ten months ago."

"Apparently, Lester was holding the information over Jack's head. And he wasn't lending Jack money. Then something happened to make Jack snap."

"And he hit Lester over the head with the briefcase." Ramsay nodded.

Beatrice said, "Lester told Jack that he was going to finally turn him in. Lester could even have just said that to toy with him some more, but Jack took him seriously. Jack lashed out at him in frustration, realized he'd taken things too far, and ran out of the house. Either Tilda saw him leave or Jack filled her in later with what happened."

Ramsay nodded. "Then Jack had the huge misfortune of seeing Shirley on the way out of the house."

"At least, Shirley saw *him*. Maybe Jack was in such a panic that he didn't even see Shirley until later."

Laura said slowly, "And Shirley was having financial problems. She couldn't even pay the mortgage on the house she was living in. That's why she decided to blackmail Jack."

"Except she wasn't really blackmailing Jack but Tilda," said Ramsay, looking grim. "And Tilda was determined to protect Jack at all costs."

Beatrice said, "I saw Jack at the church earlier today. He looked completely miserable."

"I'm sure he was," said Ramsay. "He probably didn't intend on murdering Lester. But having his mother murder Shirley in cold blood must have made him feel even worse. Then Tilda set her sights on you, Beatrice, to make sure no one besides Mellie knew about Jack's hit-and-run."

Laura said slowly, "I guess Tilda wasn't worried about Mellie saying anything?"

Beatrice shook her head. "Maybe she knew that Mellie was pretty much under her thumb and she could get her to stay in line and not call the police on Jack. Plus, Mellie seemed to be really fond of Jack."

Ramsay closed up his notebook. "Now I'd better meet up with the state police and find out how things are going with the intake process. Are the two of you okay?"

Laura said, "I'm fine—I'm more worried about Beatrice."

"No, I'm good, Laura, thank you. You should continue on your jog."

Ramsay said, "Actually, Laura, do you think you could run over to the station briefly with me so I could get your official statement?"

"Of course I can," she said.

Ramsay asked Beatrice, "Can I call Wyatt for you?"

"No, I know he had a lot of meetings this afternoon and I really am fine." She paused. "You know, I think I might give Posy a call. The shop should be about to close for the day and she and I could stop by June Bug's bakery. I think something sweet might hit the spot after a pretty sour day."

Ramsay held the door open for Laura and said, "Just remember the bright spot—the case has been solved and everything should be back to normal now."

And normal in Dappled Hills, reflected Beatrice, was pretty nice. Posy met her over at June Bug's cheerful bakery again. They both had two cupcakes—mint chocolate chip cupcakes, which were superb. And this time, June Bug herself was behind the counter instead of sending out distress calls. They happily sat, eating their sugary treats and catching up with each other as a beautiful sunset lit up the sky in pink and purple hues over the nearby mountains.

About the Author

Elizabeth writes the Southern Quilting mysteries and Memphis Barbeque mysteries for Penguin Random House and the Myrtle Clover series for Midnight Ink and independently. She blogs at ElizabethSpannCraig.com/blog, named by Writer's Digest as one of the 101 Best Websites for Writers. Elizabeth makes her home in Matthews, North Carolina, with her husband. She's the mother of two.

Sign up for Elizabeth's free newsletter to stay updated on releases:

https://bit.ly/2xZUXqO

This and That

I love hearing from my readers. You can find me on Facebook as Elizabeth Spann Craig Author, on Twitter as elizabethscraig, on my website at elizabethspanncraig.com, and by email at elizabethspanncraig@gmail.com.

Thanks so much for reading my book...I appreciate it. If you enjoyed the story, would you please leave a short review on the site where you purchased it? Just a few words would be great. Not only do I feel encouraged reading them, but they also help other readers discover my books. Thank you!

Did you know my books are available in print and ebook formats? Most of the Myrtle Clover series is available in audio and some of the Southern Quilting mysteries are. Find the audiobooks here.

Please follow me on BookBub for my reading recommendations and release notifications.

I'd also like to thank some folks who helped me put this book together. Thanks to my cover designer, Karri Klawiter, for her awesome covers. Thanks to my editor, Judy Beatty for her help. Thanks to beta readers Amanda Arrieta, Rebecca Wahr, Cassie Kelley, and Dan Harris for all of their helpful suggestions and careful reading. Thanks to my ARC readers for helping to spread the word. Thanks, as always, to my family and readers.

Other Works by Elizabeth

Myrtle Clover Series in Order (be sure to look for the Myrtle series in audio, ebook, and print):

Pretty is as Pretty Dies
Progressive Dinner Deadly
A Dyeing Shame
A Body in the Backyard
Death at a Drop-In
A Body at Book Club
Death Pays a Visit
A Body at Bunco
Murder on Opening Night
Cruising for Murder
Cooking is Murder
A Body in the Trunk
Cleaning is Murder
Edit to Death
Hushed Up
A Body in the Attic
Murder on the Ballot
Death of a Suitor

A Dash of Murder
Death at a Diner (late 2022)
Southern Quilting Mysteries in Order:
Quilt or Innocence
Knot What it Seams
Quilt Trip
Shear Trouble
Tying the Knot
Patch of Trouble
Fall to Pieces
Rest in Pieces
On Pins and Needles
Fit to be Tied
Embroidering the Truth
Knot a Clue
Quilt-Ridden
Needled to Death
A Notion to Murder
Crosspatch (late 2022)
The Village Library Mysteries in Order (Debuting 2019):
Checked Out
Overdue
Borrowed Time
Hush-Hush
Where There's a Will
Frictional Characters
Spine Tingling (late 2022)

Memphis Barbeque Mysteries in Order (Written as Riley Adams):

Delicious and Suspicious

Finger Lickin' Dead

Hickory Smoked Homicide

Rubbed Out

And a standalone "cozy zombie" novel: Race to Refuge, written as Liz Craig

CPSIA information can be obtained
at www.ICGtesting.com
Printed in the USA
LVHW050122180422
716461LV00016B/649

9 781955 395076